MURDER UNDER THE ROCK

ALI SIMPSON

The Markham Twins Investigate

MURDER UNDER ROCK

THE

Troubador Publishing Ltd
Unit E2 Airfield Business Park,
Harrison Road, Market Harborough,
Leicestershire LE16 7UL
Tel: 0116 279 2299
Email: books@troubador.co.uk
Web: www.troubador.co.uk

ISBN 9781836282839

British Library Cataloguing in Publication Data.
A catalogue record for this book is available from the British Library.

The manufacturer's authorised representative in the EU for product safety
is Authorised Rep Compliance Ltd, 71 Lower Baggot Street, Dublin D02
P593 Ireland (www.arccompliance.com).

Printed and bound in Great Britain by 4edge Limited
Typeset in 11pt Minion Pro by Troubador Publishing Ltd, Leicester, UK

For David, because this book is as much yours, as mine.

Chapters

1

The Mannar pearls

The thief didn't have a lock on his door but he wasn't overly concerned. He checked it was firmly shut before pulling the heavy dark curtains so that only a chink of the bright summer sunlight filtered through the slender gap. He turned on the lamp.

Sitting down at the old desk, he took two deep breaths. He hadn't dared look at the pearls since the night of the fire, and his heart began to beat a little faster and his palms suddenly felt sweaty. He distractedly wiped them down the front of his trousers before quietly unlocking the centre drawer. He took out a nondescript black velvet pouch.

He reached inside the bag and carefully removed the necklace, arranging it neatly on the desk in front of him.

The narrow sliver of sunlight twinkled fiercely off the diamond, ruby and emerald clasp, an intricate design of interwoven flowers. The thief wondered idly whether he could sell the clasp intact without prising out the stones first but had decided against it. He might not even sell it at all, he thought. He might keep it for a rainy-day, an insurance policy so to speak, or perhaps just tuck it away as a memento, a thrilling secret reminder that he could take out and look at whenever he wanted to relive the events of two days prior.

Either way, he had plenty of time to decide what do with it when everything had settled down and the murderer had faced justice.

From a small drawer to his right the thief took out some long, fine-nosed sewing scissors, themselves stolen. They were slender and sharp, ideal for the task in hand. There was a round bowl on the desk for bits and bobs, random erasers, paperclips, spare nibs. He tipped the contents unceremoniously onto the desk and brushed them casually to one side.

Everything was set.

He picked up the necklace, rolling one of the pearls against his front teeth. It felt reassuringly gritty. No mistaking quality.

There was a moment of hesitation. The necklace was indeed magnificent and, despite everything, he felt a momentary twinge of remorse that he was going to be the destroyer of such exquisite beauty.

But now was not the time for self-doubt or sentimentality. Any thought of coveting the Mannar pearl necklace simply for its breathtaking lustre and sublime craftsmanship was easily subsumed by the knowledge that, at this precise moment, the sum of its parts was far more valuable than its totality. They were a means to an end, a way of keeping the wolf from the door until the main prize came within the thief's grasp.

To covet. What a wonderfully biblical verb for something so singularly unchristian. A yearning to possess, a longing to take something that doesn't belong to you. Even though he wasn't a believer, there was comfort in knowing that, while Exodus 20:17 made mention of coveting your neighbour's house, wife, servant or ox, there was nothing specifically in the Bible about pearls.

Anyway, he reasoned to himself, it wasn't like a plain gold ring or a silver cigarette case, or any of the other trinkets he'd stolen in the past, easily and untraceably handed on to a myriad of unsavoury contacts willing to dispose of valuables for a tiny percentage. As a single piece of jewellery, the Mannar pearl necklace was irreplaceable and utterly unique and thus completely unsaleable.

Five strands, forty pearls per strand, graduating from the smallest at the back near the clasp to the most spectacular ones at the front of the drop, the central black pearl on each strand the most valuable of all.

Gently placing one strand between his forefinger and thumb, he deftly positioned the tip of the scissors between the first two pearls and, with a short exhalation of breath, cut the silk cord.

Each pearl was expertly knotted on both sides and he worked quickly but methodically, snipping and pulling the silk until each pearl was loose, placing them gently one by one into the bowl as they became free.

He cut around the last pearl and added it to the others. He scooped up the discarded pieces of silk, rolling them into a ball and placing it carefully into his trouser pocket. He made a mental note to drop it over a hedge or garden wall next time he went for his morning constitutional.

Stop. What was that? The thief froze, his eardrums quivering to an indistinct but familiar sound. Shoes on tiles, faint but getting closer. He knew no one would come into the room unannounced but, nonetheless, he felt a jolt of panic.

Without thinking, he reached for the bowl of pearls but caught the edge with his cuff, bumping it slightly. It rocked then tipped and some of the pearls spilled out onto the desk. He frantically scooped them up as quickly as he could, shepherding the contents into the black velvet pouch and placing it back into the drawer.

He turned the lock, put the key in his pocket and stood up, willing his heartbeat to slow. He concentrated for a moment brushing the discarded stationery back into the bowl, setting it down in its usual place on the desk. The panic started to subside.

The deed was done.

As the footsteps got louder, he put on his most comfortable smile, turned off the lamp, drew back the curtains to let the sunlight flood in as befitted such a beautiful summer day and left the room.

Unseen, one black pearl teetered on the edge of the desk having rolled between the ink blotter and the pen stand. As the door shut behind him, the pearl dropped onto the floor and came to rest unnoticed between the chair leg and the corner of the rug.

2

A murder is discovered

Publican Frank Fogwill was sleeping fitfully, dreaming about Margery. Unfortunately for Frank, Margery was not his wife.

Frank's wife Edna was sleeping soundly beside him, after thirty years of marriage, the sharp rasping of her snores hardly registering.

Margery Shepherd was the drayman's daughter and, having recently turned twenty-one and apparently not caring for a job in retail or service or anything else so demeaning, had been forced by her father to help him with his deliveries until she could find a respectable way of bringing money into the household that she found agreeable.

Every Monday and second Thursday, Thomas Shepherd and his arthritic horse, perhaps inappropriately called Charger, negotiated their cart down the steep road to The Ketch Inn.

The precarious journey, as perilous going up as it was coming down, was a constant source of worry to Frank. With the thatch of the inn almost at a level with the roadway as it flattened out at the bottom of Smugglers' Cove Road, Frank had frequent nightmares about one of the heavy barrels rattling loose and careering down the steep slope and straight through his roof. Mind you, taking the positives he had thought in one of his more unchristian moments, perhaps it might come through the bedroom ceiling and land on Edna.

Ever thought about getting one of those new motorised delivery vans? Frank had once said to Thomas, but Thomas had roundly pooh-poohed the idea. He fondly stroked his horse's head. *Mebbe, but not till you've gone to the glue factory, eh old girl?*

Despite his misgivings, Frank Fogwill's attitude to his regular beer delivery had improved significantly with the arrival of Margery on the round.

In Frank's eyes, she was everything Edna was not. Statuesque and pretty, if in a rather obvious way. She favoured new celebrity magazines and always fashioned her blonde hair into the most recent styles and wore pretty frocks despite, and much to her obvious chagrin, being forced to cover them up with the heavy leather apron that her father insisted she wear.

Alongside her good looks, she was also remarkably strong, which Frank found strangely appealing, and he had spent many happy moments watching the muscles on her brown arms flex as she hauled the barrels down into his cellar with apparently very little effort.

In his dream, Frank was in the beer cellar with Margery, who had conveniently stumbled over a barrel in the dark and fallen against him. Pleasingly, Frank realised he was naked and the feelings Margery's buxom figure and leather apron gave him as they were pressed against his bare skin could best be described as titillating.

Just then, and obviously intent on squashing his happiness as much in his dreams as in reality, Edna appeared at the bottom of the steps. Her face was like an angry wasp and she was slamming her fists against the heavy wooden hatchway, shouting *Frank, Frank*. Frank's ardour cooled almost instantly.

Frank roused slightly but the shouting remained. He sat up, now fully awake. There it was again. *Frank, Frank.* He then heard the sound of frantic pounding and realised it wasn't Edna in his dream, someone was actually beating on the door of the inn.

Edna had also stirred, sitting up, her curlers slightly askew and her eyes unattractively gummy with sleep.

'What in hell's teeth!' exclaimed Frank, jumping out of bed and deftly pulling on his trousers over his nightshirt. Fixing his braces, he grabbed his boots from the corner of the room and rushed down the steep steps in his stockinged feet. As he raced down the hallway, he glanced at the clock above the bar. Twenty-four minutes past one.

He wrenched open the door to the sight of Nelly Crouch on the step, frantically banging on the frame. Nelly, the housemaid at Rockcliffe House, was dressed in a long white night dress with her coat thrown carelessly over the top and her boots unlaced. Her wiry red hair was wild around her shoulders and there was a look of panic on her plain face.

'Oh, thank God!' she exclaimed, grabbing at Frank's arm. 'Come quickly, Frank. The house is on fire!'

Frank struggled into his boots and followed Nelly out of the door.

The Ketch Inn was on one side of the small crescent-shaped cove, Rockcliffe House on the other, the cove itself being a small bite out of a much larger bay. A dirt track hugged the coastline as it curved between the two largest properties, passing a scattering of tiny fisherman's cottages and smaller houses on the foreshore.

As he ran down the track behind Nelly, Frank could see flames licking up the nearest side of Rockcliffe House. The thatch at one end of the property was well alight , the flames starting to race across the ridge and threatening to engulf the whole roof. Black smoke was belching into the still summer night air and Frank could taste burning wheat reed at the back of his throat as he breathed in and out heavily. He wasn't used to running.

There was a general hubbub of alarmed voices as most of the residents of the nearby properties came out to see what was happening. Men were shouting and running towards the fire, many of the women holding back small children who had been awoken by the commotion or cradling little babies in their arms.

Frank saw Jacob, his potboy, emerging from the nearest cottage and he ran over to grab him by the sleeve.

'Jacob, run up to The Willows, ask Mr Ball to call the fire brigade. Chop Chop.' Jacob stood transfixed for a moment looking at the flames, and Frank shook him to rouse him out of his stupor.

'NOW boy' he shouted as loudly as he could, spraying spit on the young man's face. Jacob jumped back, startled, turned on his heels and started to run up the hill. *I might as well have a headless chicken for a potboy*, thought Frank as he turned back towards the burning house.

Edward Keane and a few of the other fishermen had just

reached the scene and some of them were forming a chain to carry buckets of water up from the sea to the house, grateful that the tide was in.

As Frank arrived he saw William Neck, the handyman, emerging from the door nearest the flames. His face and hands were already black with soot and he was holding a small hatchet. Seeing Frank, he ran over.

'Frank, we need more water,' he shouted. 'I'm trying to get those timbers cut back but we need to put the flames out first.' With that, he raced back into the building.

'Let's get the pump,' Frank shouted to the nearest man and together they ran down to the old Excise Boatman's cabin. Long abandoned, it now acted as a general store for the local fishermen, housing odd pieces of equipment, discarded nets and lobster pots.

Given the numerous thatched buildings nearby, someone a few years ago had added a pump to the store cupboard in the unlikely event of a fire. While many at the time had dismissed the idea as expensive and pointless, Frank was mightily relieved to see it still there, propped up unused in the corner of the store.

They dragged the pump and hose out and, within minutes, had rigged it up. Several of the fishermen broke the bucket line and helped to pull the heavy equipment up towards the house.

Jacob arrived back and headed for Frank who was holding the nozzle of the hose up towards the thatch.

'The fire brigade are on the way,' he said breathlessly, 'and the police too.'

Seeing the strain on Frank's face from holding the heavy equipment, Jacob added, 'Here, let me take that.'

Frank smiled. Perhaps Jacob wasn't such a waste of space after all.

As he handed the hose over to Jacob, William Neck emerged again from the side of the building, putting his head in his hands and coughing up sooty spit onto the ground.

The sound of a bell was getting louder and, within a few minutes, the assembled crowds were relieved to see the new Merryweather fire engine appear at the base of the steep hill road and drive along the dirt road purposefully towards Rockcliffe House, followed soon after by a police car driven by Sergeant Temple.

As the firemen worked to extinguish the fire, Sergeant Temple, Frank, William, Edward, Jacob and the rest of the fishermen gathered together a safe distance away from the house. Some of their wives and mothers and older children joined the group, all watching in stunned silence.

Within ten minutes, the flames appeared to be losing their grip on the house and, to everyone's relief, were eventually extinguished altogether. All that remained were some thin columns of wispy white smoke that rose lazily from the wet thatch, the burnt fragments of reed drifting down onto the solemn, upturned faces like black snow.

Frank saw Nelly standing off to one side and went over to put a reassuring arm around her shoulder. Her face, which had been panic-stricken when he'd first seen her, now just looked lost and confused.

He scanned the crowd.

'Have you seen Miss Carmody and Miss Watcombe?' he asked.

Nelly looked back at him, tears washing ugly tracks down her smoke blackened cheeks.

'Miss Carmody's away from home today,' she replied. 'But I haven't seen Miss Watcombe.' She dry-hiccupped some tears. 'Oh Lord, I think she's still in there.'

Frank ran over to Sergeant Temple, who was already taking a statement from Edward, a look of concentration on his grim face as he licked his pencil and wrote in his notebook.

'Fred,' whispered Frank close to his ear, putting a hand on the Sergeant's arm. 'No one's seen Miss Watcombe.'

There was a moment of silence. The two men exchanged a worried look.

Seeing William standing nearby, still holding the hatchet, Fred Temple signalled over to him.

'Here, lad,' he gestured to William, 'come with me. Frank, Ed, you too.'

The four men walked silently in a line up the short path to the side door and went inside the smouldering building, oblivious to the terrible scene that was about to confront them.

3

Intrigue over the breakfast table

It promised to be another gin clear day, and the early morning sun was already filtering through the net curtains of the dining room at Laburnum Villas, Wellesmead, Torquay.

As he did every morning, Dr John Markham was sitting down to breakfast with his daughters, Catherine and Eleanora, known as Kitty and Nora to their close acquaintances.

To the untrained eye, the Markham twins were indistinguishable, one from the other, both tall, pretty and dark-haired. Kitty and Nora couldn't see the similarity themselves however, and didn't really understand how so many people could muddle them up. Kitty was at least a whole half inch taller than her younger sister, and Nora's feet were at least two sizes bigger.

Nora got up to freshen her teacup from the pot and picked up the early edition of the Wellesmead and Barnswood Examiner from the sideboard.

John was much happier with the national broadsheets but his daughters and their housekeeper, Mrs Lockhart, preferred the local paper. Lots of juicy titbits about people they might know. If we want to be proper detectives, Kitty had said to Nora under the bedcovers one night, we need to know who's who and what's what and where's where. Ears open, eyes peeled.

Mrs Lockhart particularly liked the Births, Marriages and Deaths notifications, known to all as hatched, matched and dispatched. It was always a source of interest for her to know who, among her vast array of acquaintances that called the quiet suburb of Wellesmead home, was coming and going, literally and metaphorically.

If truth be told, the Wellesmead and Barnswood Examiner did not usually have the most inspiring front pages, favouring small text, turgid prose, dull photographs and dry adverts that offered sensible facts without the need for any creative flourishes whatsoever. In recent days, the paper had told its readers there was a dispute brewing about whether or not to put in a tram line between the clock tower and the sea front parade, that Devonshire Lass Ices had opened a new refreshment kiosk at Northcliffe beach and that Silverado, the baker's horse, had retired and Mr Narracott had got a new motorised delivery van. That story was certainly the talk of Wellesmead and caused general excitement for a while.

However, today, the front page of the paper was dominated by a large photograph of an elderly woman and a headline, in forty pitch, that shouted 'Murder!'

John tutted quietly. Honestly, sensationalist nonsense to use an exclamation mark in a newspaper headline. If he ever saw an exclamation mark on the front of The Times he would write a very stern letter to the Editor.

'Oh my goodness,' Nora exclaimed, holding up the front page so the others could see. Kitty's eyes widened in disbelief but John was not surprised, having received an early morning call from David Arbuthnot with the whole story.

Nora began to read out loud.

Roger Blake, Lead Reporter,

The usual quiet of Smugglers' Cove Road was greatly disturbed early this morning and the peaceful law-abiding inhabitants roused to a state of intense alarm and terror by one of the most frightful tragedies that human devilment could countenance. A crime so heinous that only a fiend disguised as a man could perpetrate.

It has been reported that Miss Agnes Watcombe of Rockcliffe House has been found brutally slain in her own home. A neighbour described Miss Watcombe as a 'gentle soul of independent means.' The crime was only discovered after local men had extinguished a fire that had already destroyed part of the house.

Laburnum Villas was less than half a mile from Smugglers' Cove Road.

'Was she one of your patients, papa?' asked Nora.

John licked some marmalade off his finger, thinking to himself that he must speak to his daughters about still calling him papa like their French mother had taught them. They were now quite grown up so perhaps Father would be more appropriate?

'No, not Miss Watcombe herself although I do look after some of her staff,' he replied. 'I think someone said she'd been with old Dr Wilde when she lived over in Brixham and didn't want to change when she came to Wellesmead.'

Kitty looked up. 'Were you there, papa, last night at Rockcliffe House?'

As the closest doctor to the scene, she was hoping he'd say yes. Didn't a physician have to be present to confirm a body was actually a dead body and not a body that just looked dead?

'No, Dr Arbuthnot was,' John replied, obviously to Kitty's disappointment. 'I was already out. Mrs Pruitt called. She was having trouble with Dorothy Choake so I said I'd go along to help out.'

Given Mrs Pruitt, the local midwife, also owned a beef and dairy farm and was adept at extricating awkward calves using ropes and pulleys, Kitty found it hard to believe she had ever had any trouble birthing a human baby so it must have irked her considerably to have to ask for the doctor's assistance. She decided not to ask her father if Mrs Pruitt had thought about using ropes and pulleys on Dorothy Choake.

John absentmindedly cleaned his glasses on the edge of the tablecloth.

He was secretly relieved. He had seen enough violent and unnatural death in the field hospitals of Artois, Verdun and Arras to last him several lifetimes and, while he had been quite put out to have to leave the warmth and comfort of his bed in the dead of night, he was now thankful he had.

Mrs Pruitt had called only forty minutes before an out-of-breath policeman had arrived at the side door of Laburnum Villas, banging furiously and waking Mrs Lockhart to see if the doctor was free to attend the scene of a murder.

Learning he was already out on an emergency call, the harassed young constable rushed off, eventually finding Dr Arbuthnot at home a mile away.

'Well, all's well that ends well, at least for Dorothy,' John continued. 'I delivered a beautiful baby boy just after two o'clock this morning.'

He paused, hoping for some dramatic effect.

'And then a beautiful baby girl at two thirty! No idea she was expecting twins. She seemed happy enough but I think Ted had a bit of shock when I went and told him.

'Just like your mother and I when you girls came along,' he reminisced, and Kitty reached over and patted his hand.

'But look on the bright side, papa, you got twice the amount of joy.'

John laughed. 'More like twice the amount of trouble.'

Nora turned her attention back to the newspaper and continued to read.

Your local reporter has been at the scene of the murder since the early hours and one local, who did not wish to be named, says he was in the room when the murder was discovered. He says Miss Watcombe was found on the floor with a deep gash across her throat, the right side of her head was smashed in and her right leg and other parts of her body were burned. The same witness reported a strong smell of gasoline pervading the charred remains of the Honeysuckle Room, the grim scene of the diabolical act.

The police have advised your Wellesmead and Barnswood Examiner reporter that they are confident of making an arrest imminently.

As Nora read, Kitty studied the photograph that dominated the front page. It was a studio portrait of an elderly lady, probably in her late seventies or early eighties, dressed in a slightly old-fashioned blouse with a high lace collar. Despite her age, her bright, fine eyes and delicate features beneath the wrinkles hinted that once, a long time ago, she must have been very beautiful.

But it was not her face that particularly caught Kitty's attention. It was the magnificent pearl necklace she was wearing. It looked expensive. Multiple strands of graduated creamy pearls with a large black pearl at the bottom drop of each strand.

Kitty's eyes lit up.

'Nora, wouldn't it be delicious to have a proper crime to investigate?' she exclaimed, pulling her silk wrap theatrically over her face like the cloak of a vaudeville villain.

'I bet it was a burglary gone wrong,' she said in a hushed tone. 'The brave Miss Watcombe fought to save her precious pearls, given to her by a jilted lover, and then paid with her life as the dastardly fiend fled the scene.'

She laughed but stopped when she saw her father's exasperated expression.

'Kitty, please. This isn't one of your silly detective adventures. This isn't a lost cat, it's murder. That poor woman has lost her life.'

'You're right, father, sorry,' said Kitty, suitably admonished. 'But our detective work isn't silly. We did some first-class investigating yesterday to find Lockie's purse.'

Kitty launched into an explanation of their most recent success, the details of which they had not yet had an opportunity to share with their father.

'She was in a terrible state in the afternoon. She went to pay the milkman and couldn't find her purse anywhere.

'Nora took a full statement, you know the sort of thing – where she'd been, when, who she'd met. She said she'd been into town so we retraced her steps along the High Street. We interviewed Mr Fox in the haberdashers and he distinctly remembered Lockie taking her purse out to pay for some buttons but Miss Smith in the Post Office said she looked a bit distracted when she was buying her stamps and had to pay for them with a few coins she had in her pocket.'

Nora joined in. 'Kitty then said she must have lost it somewhere between the two, so the only logical place it could be was by the wool shop. Well guess what, papa? We went in and there it was! Mrs Clark said a Good Samaritan had found the purse outside and brought it to her for safe keeping until the owner hopefully realised it was missing and came to reclaim it.'

'And what about Horus?' Kitty added before her father could speak. 'We traced him all the way from Stanford Hall to the park by following the white hairs caught on bits of wire and under fences.'

John had actually witnessed the denouement of that particular spectacle himself, shuddering as he remembered the scene.

He had been walking home from treating Mr Gulley's ulcerated leg when he'd seen Kitty and Nora at the edge of the park, a rather grand name for the unprepossessing patch of rough grass between the vicarage gardens and the church.

They were staring up at a tall sycamore, waving their arms and shouting encouragement to young Arthur Westacott who was swinging alarmingly in the tallest branches with what later transpired to be Horus, Lady Atkins-Chatto's Persian cat, stuffed unceremoniously down the front of his cricket jumper.

'Indeed,' replied John, raising his eyebrows. 'And Mrs Lockhart lost a perfectly good piece of pollack to the rescue effort I seem to remember.'

'Well, Lady Atkins-Chatto told us Horus was particularly partial to pollack,' explained Nora, 'and we needed something tasty so Arthur could get close enough to grab him.'

'Goodness knows what would have happened if Arthur had fallen. Honestly, girls, being the direct cause of the death of the Chief Constable's son would have been extremely hard to explain.'

'But he didn't, did he?' replied Kitty with total, incontrovertible accuracy.

John sighed. He knew he would never win this argument. Kitty and Nora had grown into kind and intelligent young women but they were also remarkably determined and logical in their reasoning. How like Caroline they were becoming, he thought. They certainly had her fierce French spirit.

'Catherine, Eleanora,' John said in his sternest voice, peering over his glasses, looking from one of his daughters to the other and back again.

'Being a detective is not a suitable hobby for any young lady and it is most assuredly not an appropriate career choice.'

'But father,' Kitty said, rather peeved. 'Lady Atkins-Chatto gave us two shillings each for finding Horus.'

'And I pay each of you ten shillings a week on top of your allowance to become useful members of society by working in the surgery. So, I'll hear no more of such nonsense and certainly no more about a murder that needn't concern you.'

John's surgery was open every day, Monday to Saturday, in the annex to Laburnum Villas. Patients came in for appointments in the morning and, in the afternoon, he went on his round of home visits. His receptionist, Mrs Carmichael, worked every day, making appointments and answering the telephone. Kitty helped with the paperwork, being quite a methodical young woman, filing, reconciling receipts and looking after the accounts while Nora helped Hester in the dispensary, managing the medicines and medical supplies.

John took out his pocket watch and glanced at the time, folding up his newspaper and getting to his feet.

'I've got appointments to get to. Mr Payne's chilblains have flared up again and Mr Mackie's sinuses won't syringe themselves. Nora, I've told Hester you'll help her in the dispensary today, that medicines audit won't do itself. Kitty, there's a pile of receipts on my desk ready for sorting and filing.'

He picked up the last crumbs of toast and popped them in his mouth, stopping behind each of his daughters to kiss the top of their heads affectionately as he did every morning before leaving the room.

Kitty picked up the local paper and looked intently at the article that Nora had read out loud as she spooned kedgeree into her mouth absent-mindedly. Nora helped herself to another slice of toast and jam and the girls ate in companionable silence for a few moments.

Kitty looked up.

'What?'

'Nothing.'

There was a pause. 'Do you fancy going for a walk before work?' Nora asked with a secret smile that only her twin would notice had a hint of devilment in it.

We aren't going to get involved, the smile said, just take a look.

'Yes, let's!' replied Kitty enthusiastically.

4

Norris goes for a walk

As they did every morning after breakfast, Kitty and Nora picked up the empty plates and stacked them untidily on the empty tureens. Tucking the newspaper under her arm, and balancing the cups, saucers and cutlery precariously on top of the pile, Kitty followed her sister with the breakfast detritus while Nora opened the doors on their way.

Elsie Lockhart was bustling about and, reassuringly, the kitchen had its usual air of organised chaos.

Mrs Lockhart didn't believe in wasting valuable time doing only one job at a time, so was darting back and forth around the kitchen as if some terrible fate would befall her if she stood still, even for a moment.

A ham for dinner was sitting on the marble meat slab, half studded with cloves and two large pots were bubbling away on the stove. By their colour and consistency, the girls assumed one was pea soup and the other a pan of jamming strawberries. Sheets of newspaper on the old kitchen table were covered haphazardly with pea husks and discarded leaves and ends of strawberries, ready to go to the compost heap. In the corner, the laundry board was set up ready for simultaneous ironing.

Having witnessed first-hand her adeptness at the dark art of household task juggling, Dr Markham had once said, 'goodness, Mrs Lockhart, if you ever get fed up being our housekeeper, you could always take your plate-spinning act to the local circus!'

Elsie Lockhart was easily as round as she was tall, which wasn't very tall at all, and the twins, who had grown willowy like their mother, towered over her. She smiled up at Kitty as she put the dirty crockery into the sink with a clatter.

On the floor next to the oven was a candlewick bedspread that had been folded and roughly sewn together, padded with old towels and fashioned into a lumpy cushion. On the cushion was Norris, Mrs Lockhart's bucolic pug.

Norris lifted his round black eyes slightly when he saw Kitty and Nora, wrinkling his already wrinkled forehead, but his chin stayed firmly planted on his outstretched paws.

The twins had always thought it strange that Mrs Lockhart had decided to call her dog after her late husband, by all accounts a rather dour Scot who had died at the Battle of Paardenberg over thirty years before. But, to anyone looking at the little framed wedding photograph she kept on her bedside table, it was probably understandable.

Norris Lockhart (the man not the dog) had been similarly short of leg and stocky of build, with dark button eyes and a rather squashed nose. Perhaps Elsie Lockhart saw her husband every time she looked at the rather unappealing but loyal little pug and it gave her some comfort.

'Have you seen the paper, Lockie?' asked Kitty, taking it from under her arm and holding up the photograph of Agnes Watcombe.

'Yes Kitty,' Mrs Lockhart replied, taking the paper from her and inspecting the picture closer. 'Such a terrible shame, something so awful to happen to such a lovely old lady and in Wellesmead too. What's the world coming to? Are we all to be murdered in our beds? Are there crazed vagrants hiding in the shrubbery just ready to strike down respectable people like us?'

'I don't think that's likely,' said Nora matter-of-factly, picking up and nibbling at a strawberry that had escaped the pot and had been nestling unseen among the discarded stalks. 'It's a fact that most murderers are known to their victims, did you know that?'

Mrs Lockhart chose to ignore her.

'Mind you,' she added, going back to the stove to vigorously stir the soup, 'nothing would surprise me at that house. Now, I'm not one to gossip, as you know, but that poor old dear was a fool to herself. Always taking in some waif and stray or another, never saw a bad bone in anyone and look where that's got her. Jean Carmody's brother, he's a bad lot and no mistake. Why Miss Watcombe would even think about giving him a job is beyond me.'

By now, she was in full flow.

'And then there's that flighty housemaid, Nelly something or other. I heard she's stepping out with one of the fishermen down at the cove, a really rough sort, Jed or Ed or Ted I think he's called. The fishmonger said you needed to count your fingers if you ever shook hands with him!'

She looked at the girls conspiratorially for a moment.

'And the less said about Jean Carmody herself the better. I'm too much of a good Christian woman to speak ill of anyone but, mark my words, she's no better than she ought to be.'

'Ooh, interesting,' said Kitty, putting her hand on Mrs Lockhart's arm. 'What do you mean?'

Mrs Lockhart brushed her hand away.

'Never you mind Kitty.' She paused then added, 'let's just say, no respectable staff would have the airs and graces she does, swanning about like she doesn't have a care in the world. Apparently poor Miss Watcombe absolutely doted on her and, grant you, she's moderately attractive but wears far too much lipstick and rouge for my liking. It's not seemly. Betty Allen said she'd even seen her with painted nails once. Perhaps she needs to remember she's the cook, not the Lady of the Manor.'

She looked around furtively, as if she suspected spies had secreted listening devices behind the rows of bottled fruit.

'I also heard she's had any number of *men friends*,' she whispered the last two words with added emphasis in case the obvious inference had passed Kitty and Nora by.

'Maybe she even murdered Miss Watcombe herself so she could steal her silver and run off to live a life of sin with one of her paramours.'

Nora considered this scenario for a moment.

'But if she's the cook, why didn't she just add some toadstools to her soup or slip a bit of rat poison into her cocoa?'

Mrs Lockhart, who preferred a good romance novel to a detective story, didn't care for Nora's reasoning. With one final stir of the soup, she turned back to the ham and started stabbing it with even more cloves than was probably good for it.

'Well, who knows what happened? I'm sure someone will be caught soon and then we can all sleep easier in our beds.' She glanced at the big kitchen clock. 'Now, don't you girls have work to do?'

Kitty looked at Nora and Nora looked at Kitty.

'Yes, but we thought we'd take Norris out for a walk first.'

'Whatever for?' Elsie Lockhart asked with a confused shake of her head.

'We know you love him, Lockie, but he's starting to look quite tubby. You're overindulging him and it can't be doing him any good. The other day when I came in he was eating a huge bowl of cold rice pudding! Anyway, Nora and I read about the benefits of keeping your pets healthy and active, so we've decided Norris could do with a fitness regime.'

Norris, who had drifted off in the warmth of the kitchen, opened his eyes when he heard his name and wondered why everyone was staring at him.

Mrs Lockhart admitted to herself that her pug *was* starting to look decidedly round, his little belly now almost scraping the floor when he walked, and she did worry about his heart being under such strain. She had tried to ignore him when he pleaded for the scrapings from the dinner plates but she had a difficult time refusing him when he looked at her with such large, sad eyes. Her late husband, God rest his soul, was partial to left-overs too.

'Well, if you're sure?' she said to Nora. 'But don't overexert him. Slowly to start with and we'll see how he goes.'

'Thanks Lockie,' Kitty said, kissing Mrs Lockhart on the cheek. 'Now get away with you,' she replied, batting Kitty away, always a little embarrassed by such obvious signs of affection.

'You'll need a lead, I think I've got one somewhere,' she added, rummaging in a drawer of miscellaneous kitchen knick-knacks, elastic bands, dishcloths, jam papers and mismatched utensils. 'Ah, here it is,' she said, extricating a rather dog-eared looking leather strap from behind a packet of paper fairy-cake cases.

*

The walk from Laburnum Villas to Glencoe, the home of their immediate neighbour Sir Charles Westacott, was less than two minutes. Out of the scullery door, across the lawn, past the tennis court, around the side of the swimming pool and out of the front gate.

They rang the bell and waited. Moments later, the door was opened by Miss Davey, Sir Charles Westacott's housekeeper.

Constance Davey was very tall and angular, with a narrow face, pointy nose and long fingers that had always reminded the twins of a witch. Her hair was scraped back as usual into such a severe bun that they often wondered if she found blinking awkward. There was a rumour that she'd done something shadowy for the Government in the war, and her unbendable military bearing suggested that might be true but, if asked, her pursed lips became even more pursed, if that were even possible, so no one ever asked twice.

She had a permanent expression of dissatisfaction with life and wore her ubiquitous thick stockings, impenetrable cardigan and flowery cotton apron like a suit of armour against the world.

It was also rumoured she never smiled but Kitty and Nora knew that was not *always* true. Before she died, their mother said she'd once even seen Constance Davey laugh, just a little, when she had come over to Laburnum Villas to celebrate the end of the war with Mrs Lockhart and a rather fine bottle of Dr Markham's homemade rhubarb wine.

Despite her less than convivial countenance, Kitty and Nora liked her very much.

'Good morning, Miss Davey,' Kitty said, putting on her most charming smile. 'Isn't it a beautiful day?'

Miss Davey pursed her lips until they were almost invisible and her eyes narrowed to their most menacing, none of which seemed to have any effect on Kitty Markham's cheerful expression.

'We're taking Norris for a walk. Lockie's bunions are playing her up,' she added, as if an explanation was needed.

Kitty picked up Norris and held him out unceremoniously in front of her as if to prove their point. He struggled for a moment but quickly resigned himself to his part in this subterfuge, staring unblinkingly at Miss Davey as if to say *it's nothing to do with me.*

Miss Davey knew the trials Elsie Lockhart had with her bunions better than anyone. The neighbouring housekeepers played bingo together in the church hall every second Thursday and Elsie had never been shy of sharing her medical woes. Miss Davey thought that probably came from living with a doctor.

But Miss Davey seriously doubted inflamed bunions had anything to do with whether or not Elsie Lockhart would be taking Norris for a walk. As far as Miss Davey was aware, the furthest Norris walked was from the scullery door to the potting shed and back again, and then only under extreme protest. Miss Davey didn't even know Elsie owned a lead for him.

'We wondered if Arthur would like to come with us?' Nora added.

'I'm not sure that would be a good idea,' Miss Davey replied slowly, remembering the last time Arthur had come home from a seemingly innocent walk with Kitty and Nora, his best cricket jumper reeking of fish and covered in cat hairs.

'Sir Charles has arranged for a tutor to come over to help Master Arthur with his mathematics before term starts. He'll be here at eleven.'

Sadly for Sir Charles, on his marriage to Arthur's mother, he learned that his newly adopted son was highly intelligent and almost totally uneducatable in any meaningful sense.

To sports-mad Arthur, mathematics was only relevant in helping him calculate his required run rate per over, history only as necessary as it took him to look back at the Ashes statistics since 1882 and the less said about English, Latin and the Classics the better. The only subject he had any time for was chemistry, endlessly fascinated by the combining of chemicals, making invisible ink, growing borax crystals and creating baking soda and vinegar volcanoes. Sir Charles had once said, after a particularly dangerous experiment that nearly blew up the garage, 'Arthur, my dear boy, I don't think Alchemy is a recognised degree at Cambridge!'

After his wife's death, Sir Charles had taken no time in sending Arthur to a public school in Wiltshire where, he hoped, some academic prowess could be instilled in him, either by persuasion or perhaps more forceful means. Sadly, so far, it hadn't.

Kitty wasn't to be deterred.

'Oh, we aren't going too far. We've got to get back to the surgery by ten thirty at the latest anyway. Probably just to the Green for a quick pootle around. Poor little Norris, his legs are far too stubby to walk any distance anyway, but he does need some exercise. You're getting awfully rotund, aren't you Norris?' she said, playfully wiggling Norris in her arms much to his obvious alarm.

'And you know what Arthur's like,' added Nora. 'A bit of fresh air will do his powers of concentration the world of good before he has to knuckle down to his studies.'

Kitty and Nora stared unblinkingly at Miss Davey, willing her to disagree.

Miss Davey hesitated. 'Well, I suppose it would be all right,' she said reluctantly, wishing she could find a good reason to disagree with Nora's obvious logic, 'but only for half an hour, no longer. Come in and wait in the drawing room. I'll go and fetch Master Arthur, I think he's upstairs.'

'Excellent,' said Nora.

The drawing room at Glencoe was always gloomy. The room faced full west and, when the sun did eventually move around to the back of the house, Miss Davey promptly closed the curtains to prevent the rugs from fading.

The room itself was pleasant enough though. Two large, overstuffed sofas offered a comfortable place to sit and a large fireplace at one end made the room cosy in winter despite the aspect.

Kitty and Nora had been in the room many times and what always fascinated them most was the sheer number of framed photographs that jostled for space along the walls and on every available surface. The common denominator in all the photographs was that Sir Charles was in every single one.

As he was the Chief Constable of Devonshire, a role that gave him almost equal social standing in the area, at least in his eyes, with the Lord Lieutenant, the High Sheriff and the Mayor, it was unsurprising that he should be involved in so many photographic opportunities, but the fact that he liked to frame and display them all so blatantly did rather make Kitty and Nora wonder about his character. After one visit to Glencoe, they had heard their mother say to their father in a hushed tone, 'so much narcissism feels a bit unseemly, don't you think John?'

Many of the photographs were recent, showing Sir Charles in his tunic and medals, others older before Sir Charles took office. As they waited for Arthur, the girls passed a few minutes perusing the photographs, many of which were helpfully labelled.

Sir Charles Westacott, Deputy Chief Constable, hands out prizes to the winners of the Barnswood Swimming Club Under 11's Sea Races 1926.

SIR CHARLES WESTACOTT, CHIEF CONSTABLE, AND ALDERMAN HUGH BARRACLOUGH, CUTTING THE RIBBON AT THE OPENING OF THE NEW CONCERT HALL IN MANNINGHAM WAY 1928.

The Novus Initium Society Annual Dinner Dance 1900

Kitty glanced at the photograph showing Sir Charles as a young man.

Now in later life he had a rather lined, care-worn face with sagging jowls, heavy eyelids and a receding grey hairline but, back in 1900, even Kitty had to admit Sir Charles, or just Charles as he was then, was rather handsome in black tie and tails, a full head of luxuriant dark hair swept away from his tanned forehead and his jawline looking firm and commanding. *Who knew he had once been so dashing?* she thought idly.

Both Kitty and Nora looked up as the drawing room door opened and Arthur Westacott stuck his head around it.

At sixteen, Arthur was small for his age but what he lacked in stature he made up for in having a sunny personality, witty outlook on life and unbounded energy. He joked that, with his low centre of gravity and almost reckless love of danger, he was particularly adept at climbing, running, jumping and getting into tight spaces.

'Quick,' he said, 'let's go before she changes her mind.'

As they let themselves out of the ornate gate at the top of the path, Arthur turned left but stopped as the girls turned right.

'I thought Miss Davey said we were going to the Green?' he said.

Kitty smiled. 'Not today Arthur.' She paused. 'We're going to the beach.'

5

An open and shut case?

The walk down from Wellesmead to Smugglers' Cove took about fifteen minutes. The three walked along the main road as it ran parallel to the sea, all the while Kitty and Nora updating Arthur on the murder of Miss Watcombe.

As the road turned slightly inland, they passed the funicular railway upper station and took the short, unmade lane that turned back towards the water, eventually ending at a stile and the start of the steep cliff path down to the beach.

The year before, the whole town had been delighted to welcome the opening of the funicular railway, cut into the slope and taking enthusiastic holidaymakers and locals alike down to Smugglers' Cove. It was certainly a far too steep and arduous a journey for most people to make on foot. Going down was vertiginous and slippery, coming back up agony on thigh muscles and dangerous for weak hearts.

Kitty, Nora and Arthur, however, decided to save their penny fare today and walk down, passing a few early holidaymakers as they waited patiently at the top station for the funicular to arrive. Norris had become stubborn on realising that he wasn't going straight home from his trip out into the big wide world, and had refused to walk any further, so the three took it in turns to carry him down.

The cliff path weaved around alongside the rail track and, at one point, dipped underneath it before doubling back. Small children particularly liked to sit under the track and hear the rumbling of the pulleys and gears and motor as the cars passed each other just above their heads, up and down.

At the bottom station, the path turned left and most of the holiday makers who enjoyed the thrill of the journey down made their way to the beach, a wide crescent of shingle and sand with a small promenade, and a myriad of refreshment kiosks, cafes and souvenir shacks that had proliferated since the arrival of the funicular. As they stepped out of the carriage, a large 'A' board greeted them, reading 'WELCOME TO SMUGGLERS' COVE. HAVE A FUN-ICULAR-TIME!!'

Instead of turning left, Kitty, Nora and Arthur turned right onto a thin dirt track that ran along the water's edge away from the tourist beach.

Despite being called a cove, the whole bite into the bay was at least a half mile long, with the funicular at one end and The Ketch Inn dominating the headland at the other.

Underneath The Ketch Inn was a small pebble beach with a little stone fishing pier jutting out into the sea and a few small boats pulled high up onto the shingle. Even though it had an industrious, picturesque charm of its own, the discarded nets, crab pots and untidy detritus that the fishermen left behind made it much less popular with the visiting tourists. At this time of day, after the fishermen had left and before the inn opened, it was always quiet.

The landscape also became wilder and more imposing as they walked to the far end of the cove. Behind the row of fishermen's cottages, and rising vertically some fifty feet or so, was a cliff face called locally 'The Rock,' towering granite that gave the whole area a certain claustrophobic sense of rampant greenery and foreboding nature. A stand of tall trees and dense shrubbery topped the cliff, making it even more dramatic.

The trio walked in single file to start but, as the path rose and opened out slightly to a wider viewing area, they stopped side-by-side to take their first look at Rockcliffe House, 'The Rock' towering ominously behind it.

It had been a large, pretty house, with rough plastered walls and a deep thatched roof which curved attractively over a bank of long casement windows, each glazed with decorative glass and framed by dark blue shutters. Running the length of the house above the ground floor windows, a tin-roofed veranda offered some protection from the gales and rain storms, each metal archway ending on a low wall topped with stone troughs filled with flowers, patriotic geranium, alyssum and lobelia adding a splash of red, white and blue. On one end of the house there was a glass-roofed orangery that led out on to a surprisingly large lawn, despite the proximity of the sea and rocks, and edged with low shrubbery.

Now as they looked down from their vantage point about a hundred yards from the house, Kitty, Nora and Arthur could see the devastation of yesterday's fire.

Much of the thatch had been burned away, a few charred timbers all that remained of the roof and there were gaping holes under the eaves into the first floor rooms. Being a long building, the near end of the house seemed relatively unscathed but the white walls at the far end of the house were blackened from the intensity of the flames and they could see that several windows had blown out and the side door had completely fallen inward. The orangery itself had all but collapsed, the decorative metalwork buckled and twisted under the heat and large chunks of plasterwork had rained down and now littered the lawn like oddly shaped snowballs. Nora couldn't help thinking it looked like a giant used matchstick lying on its side, much of the stem intact but burned and blackened at one end.

The police had put a thin rope around the front of the house, looping it between the plant pots, tying it off on the right to a lamp post and, on the left, to a large shrub. A tall police constable was standing in front of the structure guarding the scene, his back ramrod straight, his eyes firmly to the front, deterring the inquisitive, curious or just downright ghoulish from getting any closer.

Kitty recognised the figure straightaway.

'Coo-eee,' she shouted, but they were too far away to be heard and the figure remained unmoved. They walked on until they reached the outskirts of the house where two small children, a girl of perhaps ten and a little boy of three or four, were standing in front of the police constable, staring at him unnervingly.

'Hello Jimmy,' said Nora and the young man smiled back broadly before seeming to remember his serious duty at the scene, and his young audience.

'Miss Markham, Miss Markham, Master Arthur,' he said curtly.

'Gosh, that's a bit formal, isn't it Jimmy?' replied Kitty with a smile.

'Not at all Miss,' the constable replied. 'I'm working. This is a police matter so I'll have to ask you to move along.'

He looked at the two small children. 'Right you two,' he shouted, 'I've had enough of you staring at me. Hop it!' They ran off towards a young woman who was standing outside one of the fishermen's cottages. All three disappeared inside, the door slamming behind them.

The area was quiet again and, without his young audience, the police constable relaxed and turned towards his friends.

James Keyse, Jimmy to his friends, was the great nephew of Elsie Lockhart. At twenty-two, he was a year older than Kitty and Nora and had been a police man for eight days short of nine months.

In looks, James Keyse was the antithesis of Elsie Lockhart. Tall, lithe and athletic, with a mop of corn blond hair, riotous freckles and a ready smile. What he lacked in Kitty and Nora's sophistication and social standing, he amply made up for with boyish charm and an appealing trust in human nature, attributes that had been both helpful and challenging in his chosen profession.

Having a small family and no children of her own, Elsie Lockhart was particularly fond of her great nephew and, consequently, he had spent a lot of time at Laburnum Villas growing up. Despite their physical dissimilarity, they had spent so much time together that some passing acquaintances had even thought Kitty, Nora and James were siblings.

As well as their love of swimming and tennis, the three had shared another passion growing up. The love of detective stories.

Kitty favoured Margaret Allingham and Dorothy L Sayers, seeing herself as a negotiator, the unraveller of knots, like her newest favourite Albert Campion, perhaps with a touch of the theatrical charm of Lord Peter Wimsey. Nora, on the other hand, was more measured, a watcher and waiter, a meticulous reasoner with a cool analytical brain like her own heroes, Hercule Poirot and Sherlock Holmes.

Jimmy Keyse didn't presume to have any of the qualities of his favourite characters, but he secretly loved the exoticness of Charlie Chan and Ellery Queen. Their exploits on the other side of the world seemed exciting to a young boy who had hardly ever left Torquay, let alone Devon, and who had dreamed of being a policeman since he was ten.

The three friends had spent many a long, hot afternoon in the summer, lounging by the Markham's pool or tucked up in front of the fire in the snug when the cooler, autumnal nights drew in, reading aloud from the latest book they had picked up at the library, discussing the plots and always trying to be the first to work out whodunnit.

'We didn't expect to see you here,' said Kitty, looking over Jimmy's shoulder at the front of the house. Now they were close to it, they could really see the devastating effect the fire had had. There was a glimpse of charred wallpaper through the open space where the front door had been and they could see part of a burnt away staircase. Outside, a thin layer of ash coated the flowers and grass to the front, dulling the greens, white, red and blue to a muddy grey.

'Isn't it awful?' Nora said sadly.

'Terrible,' agreed Jimmy looking back at the ruined building, reaching over and scratching Norris distractedly between the ears.

Gosh, he's heavy, Nora thought, putting Norris on the ground and flexing her arm which had gone to sleep.

'Can we take a look inside?' asked Kitty.

'Of course not Kitty,' answered Jimmy shaking his head, as if it was the daftest question he had ever been asked. 'More than my job's worth.'

'Of course, sorry.'

Jimmy sighed. 'Honestly, why nice, kind old Miss Watcombe let a wrong'un like that into her home beats me.'

'A wrong'un?'

'Oh, haven't you heard?' said Jimmy, secretly pleased that he apparently knew something that Kitty and Nora didn't. 'Before I came down here for my shift, Sergeant Blackworthy said they'd arrested Miss Watcombe's handyman, William Neck.'

'Oh,' said Nora, with a frown. 'That was awfully quick, wasn't it? They haven't even had the inquest yet. Did he confess?'

'I don't think so. I think he was protesting his innocence to everyone and anyone who would listen when they dragged him into the station. Anyway, I think they've called the inquest early for tomorrow, given the seriousness of the crime, so we'll find out more then.'

'But they must have some good evidence?' queried Kitty.

Jimmy looked pleased that, once again and in the space of five minutes, he could impress Kitty, Nora and Arthur with his intimate knowledge of the case.

'Of course,' he said, trying not to look smug. 'I don't

know the details but I heard that they found a bloody knife in his overcoat pocket and one of Miss Watcombe's silver plates wrapped in an old cloth and hidden under his bed.'

'How convenient,' said Nora with a frown.

'What do you mean, convenient, Nora?' replied Jimmy. 'Seems like he's banged to rights to me. Apparently, he'd only been released from prison two months ago. Theft of a pocket watch I think. A regular jailbird, by all accounts. In and out since he was thirteen. Mostly burglary, theft and receiving stolen goods. Once a wrong'un, always a wrong'un, I say.'

As if to seal the coffin lid on the fate of the accused himself, Jimmy remembered something else. 'Oh, and he had blood all down his trousers, and someone said his boots reeked of kerosene.'

It certainly seemed a watertight case.

Kitty paused as if something important was occurring to her.

'What about the pearls?' she asked.

'Pearls?'

'Yes, Miss Watcombe had some extremely valuable pearls. Did they find them in William Neck's possession?'

Jimmy looked perplexed. 'I don't think so or, if they did, I didn't hear about it. Perhaps he thought they were out of his league, so he just left them behind.'

'So did the police find them on the victim?'

'I don't think so.'

'So if the police didn't find them when they searched the house, where are they now?' asked Arthur innocently, much to Jimmy's exasperation.

'And if William Neck felt like that about the pearls,' Kitty interjected, 'why didn't he just steal all the silver plates and disappear off into the night?'

'And surely if there was blood on the knife and on his trousers, there would have been blood on his hands too?'

'And was there any forced entry?'

'What's with all the questions?' Jimmy replied with a little too much vigour, realising he had now exhausted his actually quite limited knowledge of the events of the previous night.

Nora scuffed the tip of her boot into a pile of ash that lay at the bottom of the white garden wall.

'I don't know, just all seems a bit predictable. A common criminal inveigles his way into the home of a wealthy spinster, carries out an apparently poorly planned and totally random murder and leaves behind damning evidence against himself for everyone to find.'

'Well, in my experience,' replied Jimmy, tapping his forehead, 'most murderers aren't too bright up here.'

Kitty laughed at her friend, not unkindly. 'Oh Jimmy, you don't have any more experience of murderers than Nora or I, not the non-fictional ones at any rate. The nearest you've come to a proper criminal is when you arrested that shoplifter last month and wasn't that just because he ran out of Bartholomew's with his pockets full of bottles of whisky and ran right into you?'

'True,' admitted Jimmy, slightly deflated. His face lightened somewhat. 'But I do have some exciting news. One of the more experienced constables is off sick with bursitis so Sergeant Pell has asked me to go to Brixham this afternoon to interview Jean Carmody.'

'The accused's sister?'

'Yes, do you know her?'

'No, not personally, but Lockie does,' said Kitty, adding to herself *by reputation*, remembering what Mrs Lockhart had suggested about the morals of Miss Watcombe's cook.

'Is she a witness or a potential accomplice?' asked Nora.

'Witness I think, but you never know. By all accounts, she was the one who persuaded poor Miss Watcombe to employ Neck in the first place, and it does seem a bit rum that she wasn't at home last night when the murder took place. I'm sure it's just a coincidence but it'll all need recording for the prosecution.'

'And defence surely?' added Arthur, and Jimmy nodded.

Kitty looked at Jimmy.

'Are you driving to Brixham?'

'No. Sergeant Temple has the police car this afternoon so I'll be going over on the bus.'

Kitty thought for a moment.

'I'll take you over if you like. It'll do Betty good to have a run out. Get her cogs turning and all that.'

Jimmy stared at Kitty, instantly wary of her motivation. He knew her too well.

'You can drive me over Kitty but you can't come in with me.'

'Of course not, I wouldn't dream of it. Just thought you might like the company and it's an awfully long way on the bus.'

It *was* a long way on the bus, Jimmy thought.

'Well, if you're sure?'

'Positive.'

Arthur glanced at his watch. 'Crikey,' he exclaimed. 'It's five past. If I'm not back by half past I'll probably never be let out of my room again. Either that or I'll be sent to school in the colonies. Come on you two.'

'Skates on then,' said Nora, scooping up Norris. 'Bye Jimmy,' she shouted over her shoulder as she and Arthur started quickly back up the path.

'See you at two o'clock outside the police station?' asked Kitty.

'Perfect, see you then.'

'Oh, Jimmy,' she added as she turned. 'Try to find out if the police have Miss Watcombe's pearls.'

Kitty waved back to Jimmy and then ran to catch up with Nora and Arthur.

As luck would have it, the funicular railway was just about to leave the bottom station when they arrived so Nora paid the 3d. for them all and they were back at the main road in five minutes.

They arrived back at their respective gates with two minutes to spare. Before they parted ways, Nora turned to Arthur.

'Arthur, I think I might have an interesting job for you later. I need to talk it over with Kitty first but, if okay, can I leave you a message in the usual place. It would mean going out after dark, if that'd be all right?'

Arthur was instantly intrigued. 'No problem. I'm sure I can climb down the wisteria from my room, I've done it before. Just let me know what you need me to do.' With a quick wave, he ran up the path to his house.

6

Betty's day out

Kitty and Nora stood by their gate and watched Arthur disappear around the side of Glencoe.

Nora turned to her older sister.

'So, what do you think?'

Kitty sighed. 'I don't know, Nora,' she admitted. 'It just feels a little bit wrong, slightly off kilter if that makes sense. Would Poirot or Wimsey or Campion have been satisfied with such an open and shut case?'

'But this isn't detective fiction you know?' Nora replied kindly, rubbing her sister's arm.

'Perhaps the norm is that the most obvious suspect actually did it. Not some vicar or butler or doctor or adopted child, but just a desperate, not too bright, criminal who isn't clever enough to hide the evidence or disappear into the night. Fiction would be awfully dull if it really was the jailbird handyman who did it, and not some criminal mastermind. Perhaps that's just not what happens in real life. Perhaps Jimmy was right after all.'

They linked arms and started to walk up the path towards the front door.

Seeing the dejected look on Kitty's face, Nora squeezed her hand.

'That doesn't mean I don't think we shouldn't dig a bit further. Could be quite a useful case, if indeed it is so clear cut, to get our teeth into even if all we do is uncover more evidence that William Neck was really the culprit after all like everyone thinks.'

She thought about Kitty's offer to drive Jimmy to Brixham.

'Did you fancy you might get a chance to speak to Jean Carmody?'

Kitty nodded.

'Hmm,' Nora pondered. 'Not sure how, and Jimmy will be angry if you do after you promised him you wouldn't.'

'What I actually said was I wouldn't go in with him, I didn't actually say I wouldn't go in at all.'

'You'll need a cover story if you want to speak to Jean.'

Kitty considered this for a moment 'How about pretending I'm a lady police detective?'

Nora laughed. 'Well, that's just plain daft. I know they have lady police officers in London, even detectives I've read, but I'm not sure Sir Charles would encourage it here. Even if he did, I suspect they'd just end up making the tea. No, you need something more believable.'

'Yes, you're right, that wouldn't work and, anyway, it would put Jimmy in a very difficult position and I'd never do that to him.' They stopped and stood in silence for a moment.

Kitty cocked her head slightly to one side, something both twins were apt to do when a thought came to them.

'What if I pretended just to be a friend of a friend of the family of Miss Watcombe, going over to offer my condolences? I can take some flowers from the garden.'

Nora considered the idea for a moment. 'Well, as a strategy, it's not too risky. Definitely worth a try.' Kitty beamed. Nothing she liked more than a bit of amateur dramatics.

'I'll park around the corner. Jimmy can go in first and do his formal interview then, when he's back at the car, I'll go and knock on the door as if it's a total coincidence. She'll never realise we're together. We can then come back here and compare notes. I'll invite him over for tennis on Sunday if he's not working.'

'You do know that Jimmy might still never speak to either of us again if you stick your beak in?'

'Don't worry,' Kitty said confidently. 'Leave Jimmy to me.'

'By the way, what is it you want Arthur to do?' Kitty added.

They went through the front door into the hall. All was quiet at Laburnum Villas.

Nora looked around to check that there was no one listening, but lowered her voice anyway, putting her face close to Kitty's.

'I thought I'd see if he wanted to get into Rockcliffe House and have a mooch around. Find some clues, uncover some evidence, that sort of thing. It would have to be after dark and he would have to get past the police guard, but I'm pretty sure he'd be up for the challenge. What do you think?'

Kitty clapped her hands, but Nora shushed her.

'Sounds right up Arthur's street,' she whispered back. 'Are you going to leave him a note in the biscuit barrel?'

Nora glanced at her watch. 'Yes, but it will have to be a bit later. Hester will skin me alive if I don't get on with that medicines audit this morning. Where are you going to say you're going this afternoon?'

'Not sure but I'll think of something. I've got filing to do first. It's so boring I'll have plenty of time to think up a convincing story. I'll also have to think up a way of getting Jimmy on side with my plan.'

'I wouldn't worry about that,' Nora replied with a smile. 'You could always twist him around your little finger.'

They returned Norris to his bed in the kitchen, something he seemed extremely grateful for after his little adventure outside the curtilage of Laburnum Villas and walked back to unlock the door to their father's surgery. Nora turning left to the dispensary and Kitty right towards her father's private study.

*

It was just before lunch when Kitty heard her father coming down the hallway towards his surgery study. He had a distinctly tuneless whistle and a repertoire of precisely two songs, *Keep On The Sunny Side* and *Stormy Weather*. One for two seasons, he'd once said with a smile. If I can find a song about spring flowers and snow I'll have the full set.

Today, Kitty was glad to hear him whistling about the sun which was a positive sign he was in a good mood.

She picked up the last piece of paper from the basket, a receipt for some medical supplies, wrote the details in the ledger and put it in the filing cabinet under the *Bills to Pay* section.

John came into the room and put his medical bag down onto the desk with a gentle thump. He always kept it in the consulting room in case he was called out on an emergency.

'Hello, papa,' said Kitty, closing the cabinet. 'Had a good morning?'

'Very good, thanks Kitty,' he replied. 'You?'

'Yes thanks,' she said, hoping he wouldn't detect the slightest falseness in her smile. Filing really was her pet hate. She held up the basket triumphantly. 'Look, all done.'

'Excellent.'

He started to busy himself around his desk, taking a few items out of his bag, so Kitty put on her brightest, most winning smile.

'Papa,' she said, 'Can I borrow Betty after lunch?'

John looked up. 'What for?'

'Well, I thought I'd take some flowers over to Myra Searle. She's staying with her grandmother in Churston Ferrers and she's been awfully unwell with bronchitis. I thought it might cheer her up.'

'Myra Searle?' The name didn't ring a bell with John.

'Yes, you remember surely?' said Kitty, although it was quite clear from his quizzical expression and furrowed brow that he absolutely didn't.

'One of my very best friends from school. Short girl, overbite. Father was a dentist in Frome. Mother was Italian.'

John thought he might be losing his marbles. He remembered a Florence Watson, an Amy Pugh, a Patricia Pateman, but not a Myra Searle, and he certainly felt he should know her from such a specific description.

'Ah yes, Myra Searle. I remember her,' he lied with as much conviction as he could muster. 'Nice girl, liked netball?'

'That's the one,' replied Kitty enthusiastically, having to suppress a smile. There was no Myra Searle and so the chance of her liking netball was literally as non-existent as her overbite.

'I don't see why not, Kitty. That's very thoughtful of you.'

Betty was John's pride and joy, a two-seater Austin Seven Coupe in black with burgundy leather.

The year before, he had been contacted by the solicitors of a distant aunt to say she had left him some money in her will. He didn't remember her clearly, except perhaps being taken to see her once or twice as a very small child by his mother and finding her whiskery chin and the smell of mothballs slightly alarming. Nonetheless, she had obviously not forgotten young John and had bequeathed him 150 pounds on her death.

Although not overly parsimonious, neither was John Markham known to be spendthrift and he had thought long and hard about what to do with the money. Despite his protestations that it would be better off saved than spent, for once in his life his daughters had persuaded him to buy something frivolous and just for him. They felt he needed cheering up with their mother, Caroline, not long passed away.

So, he went to Exeter the next day and bought Betty on a whim, paying the grand sum of 140 pounds for her, with an extra five pounds for the sliding sunroof. He gave two pounds to Kitty and two pounds to Nora for their savings and put the remaining one pound into the church collection box.

Unfortunately, John was not the sort of man to be able to spend a large amount of money on himself and he instantly felt guilty, particularly as he actually enjoyed walking between his patients and very rarely needed to drive. If truth be told, he also felt Betty was a little ostentatious to be driven around Wellesmead by the local doctor.

So Betty sat, largely undriven, in the garage at Laburnum Villas and was only taken out on very special occasions.

John, however, did find cleaning Betty cathartic. He sometimes had blue moods, usually when he thought about Caroline or if something reminded him of a particular soldier he had treated, and lost, during the war, and he found the very act of washing, polishing, waxing and buffing oddly calming. Consequently, while Betty did not see the open road as often as he might like, he prided himself on the fact that she was still as shiny as the day he drove her out of the showroom.

'She's been sitting for a while now,' said Kitty. 'It would do her good to get out. Stop her tyres from seizing up, if nothing else.'

'Of course,' replied her father, secretly pleased. It would give him the perfect excuse on Sunday to spend a few hours with his sponge and chamois leather.

'I'm actually going to Plymouth this afternoon on a bit of business, but I was going to take the train anyway. Before you go, can you tell Mrs Lockhart I'll be back for dinner?'

Before she left, Kitty thought of something else. Her father was in a good mood so, in for a penny, in for a pound.

'I don't suppose you'd let us go to Miss Watcombe's inquest tomorrow would you?'

'Absolutely not Kitty and, when I say absolutely not, I mean absolutely not. Anyway, Mrs Lockhart wants to do her annual rug beating tomorrow while the weather's fine, and I've told her you and Nora will be around to hang them up on the line and take them down again for her. I'm not having her up those steps and spraining her ankle like last year. Understood?'

Kitty touched her forelock playfully. 'Absolutely.'

Trying hard to suppress a tingle of excitement that everything else was going to plan so far, Kitty kissed her father goodbye, wished him a productive afternoon, and skipped up the stairs to her room to change.

7

In defence of the accused

As Kitty rounded the corner into Cedar Road, she could see Jimmy already waiting outside the police station.

She was five minutes late. Having sat idle for so long, Betty was initially reluctant to start and took some cajoling before she eventually turned over and, with a sigh of relief, Kitty felt the engine spring into life.

Jimmy looked very handsome in his uniform, Kitty had to admit. He really wore it well, being tall and slim and impossibly fair. People often found the juxtaposition of the uniform and his boyish good looks disarming, and he had been subjected more than once to a comment of *you know you're getting old when the policemen start to look so young.*

She pulled Betty to a stop and leant over to open the door.

'Good afternoon Constable Keyse,' she said formally. 'May I escort you to Brixham for the purposes of interviewing a key witness to a murder?'

'Very funny,' Jimmy said, struggling somewhat into the tight space, folding his long legs under so they just fitted. He took out a scrunched-up piece of paper from his pocket and flattened it out on his thigh.

'Righteo. She's staying with her sister apparently. Seaview Parade, Brixham. Number 78. I think I know where that is.'

Checking her little rearview mirror, Kitty pulled away from the kerb and headed towards Brixham.

As he rearranged his limbs to get more comfortable and looked for somewhere to put his police helmet, Jimmy glanced over his shoulder and noticed a bunch of pink and white carnations, wrapped in paper, lying on the tiny back seat.

'They're pretty. Are they for someone special?'

Never one to shy away from meeting potential conflict straight on and knowing she only had about fifteen minutes to get Jimmy onside, Kitty decided there was no time to waste.

'I'm going to give them to Jean Carmody,' she replied, keeping her eyes straight forward on the road. She almost thought she heard Jimmy's head snap around and she felt his eyes glaring at her.

'Oh no you're not.'

'Oh yes I am.'

'Oh no you're not.'

'Oh yes I am.'

'No.'

'Yes.'

Kitty slammed on her brakes and pulled Betty into the side of the road, causing Jimmy to brace himself with both hands against the dashboard.

'Jimmy,' she said firmly, turning in her seat to stare at him. 'If we carry on much longer like this, one of us is going to have to shout *he's behind you* and that would be extremely silly!'

'I told you, you're not coming in with me. It's more than my job's worth.'

'Of course not, silly,' she said. 'But I would like to speak to her. I've got a watertight plan. Surely two heads are better than one? She might tell me things she wouldn't tell you, and vice versa.'

Jimmy sighed. He knew there was little point in trying to argue with Kitty when she was obviously so determined.

'All right,' he said reluctantly. 'I'm not saying yes, but what's your plan?'

'Well, I'm going to park up nearby but not outside the house. You go in and do your interview, all above board and no chance of any repercussions for you. You come back to the car and wait, and then I'll go and knock on the door. Completely unconnected.'

'And who are you going to say you are?'

'I don't think I can be Kitty Markham, much too dangerous. Father said he looked after some of the staff over at Rockcliffe House and I checked his files. He was right and Jean Carmody is one of them. I don't want her saying, 'oh, are you any relation to Dr John Markham?'

'Good point.'

'So I'll use an alias.' She thought for a moment. 'How about Alice Archibald?' Alice was Kitty's middle name, and Archibald was her first pet cat.

'So that's your name sorted but what are you going to say when she asks why you're there?'

'I thought perhaps the granddaughter of an old acquaintance of Miss Watcombe. Not someone so close that Jean Carmody would necessarily have known of me, but someone suitably removed who might well have known Miss Watcombe, perhaps before Jean came into her employment.'

'Sounds reasonable,' conceded Jimmy, although he was obviously still not overly comfortable with the whole subterfuge.

'Honestly, Kitty,' he said, sitting back in his seat as she signalled to pull back out onto the road. 'You do know it's futile, don't you? William Neck is the guilty man. Everyone is talking about it. Even Sir Charles came down to the station yesterday with bottles of beer for each man as a thank you for solving the crime so quickly.'

'So, it doesn't matter then,' reasoned Kitty. 'What's the harm? Jean Carmody will just confirm everything you already know, that her brother murdered Miss Watcombe and that's the end of it.'

She concentrated as she steered wide passed two very slow horse-drawn carriages.

'Oh, did you find out about the pearls? Did the police collect them from the house on the night of the murder?'

'No, no mention of pearls in the evidence log and Archie, sorry Constable O'Connor, confirmed they hadn't been found and he was one of the first in the house after Sergeant Temple had secured the scene.'

'Do they have a theory, the detectives in charge?'

'They're hardly likely to tell a lowly copper like me, are they? But I did hear on the station grapevine they're saying perhaps Neck stole them before the night of the murder and has just secreted them somewhere. Perhaps in the woods behind the house.'

Kitty was dubious.

'Anyway,' she said, changing the subject. 'Do you have your questions prepared? What are you going to ask her?'

Glad of the distraction away from thinking about what could possibly go wrong with Kitty's plan, Jimmy took out his notebook.

'Mostly basic facts. How long she'd worked for Miss Watcombe, how William Neck had come to be employed by Miss Watcombe, what his background was, etcetera.'

'Is that it?'

'What do you mean?' replied Jimmy, slightly hurt.

'Jimmy, try to get under the surface a bit. Winkle out something more meaningful. Ask her about the pearls. I still think they're key. Where did Miss Watcombe keep them? Who knew how valuable they were? Had William ever seen them or commented on them? Did she have a safe? Did she and William get along? Were there any disputes between them? How many visitors came to the house and who were they? Does Miss Carmody have any men friends? Who knew she was staying at her sister's that night? Did Miss Watcombe have a will? Where is it? Does Jean know who the beneficiaries are?'

'Slow down Kitty,' Jimmy said, writing frantically. They drove in silence for a few minutes. 'Got it!'

He put his notebook down.

'And what are you going to ask her?' Jimmy asked. 'You can't let her know you know anything about the case, or that you're even interested in it.'

'Of course not. I'm just going to see if I can gain her trust and maybe she'll let her guard down and tell me something useful. Perhaps it'll be more about feelings than evidence.

Did she think William was actually capable of something as awful as brutally murdering a defenceless old woman for money?'

Ten minutes later, they found Seaview Parade, a row of pretty terraced houses one road back from the harbour. They drove slowly by, identifying number 78, then Kitty turned the corner and parked Betty in the adjacent street.

Jimmy unfurled his legs and got out of the car, stretching a little to get some feeling back into his feet. He put his head through the open side window.

'I don't know how long I'll be,' he said, 'maybe thirty minutes or so.'

Kitty gave him a big smile of encouragement. 'Don't worry, I'll still be here when you get back.'

She watched in the rear view mirror as Jimmy put on his helmet, adjusted his tunic and walked back down the side road. He turned the corner and disappeared from view.

Kitty was rehearsing her character in her head when, exactly twenty-five minutes later, Jimmy tapped on the window, making her jump.

She reached over and let him in.

'All good?'

'All good.'

Kitty checked her lipstick for at least the hundredth time, and smoothed her short, bobbed hair back, tucking it behind her ears.

She reached back in over her seat to retrieve the flowers.

'Wish me luck.'

'Good luck.'

Kitty took a deep breath to steady her nerves and walked purposefully away.

The house was narrow and pebble-dashed, with thick lace curtains at the downstairs windows. There was a small wrought iron gate and a short path to a green painted door. Kitty rang the bell and waited.

The door was opened by a lady Kitty thought was probably in her early forties. She had short mousy hair with a touch of grey, and a kind face, attractive in a solid way.

'Yes, can I help you?'

'Good afternoon, I wonder if I could possibly to speak with Miss Carmody?'

'I'm Miss Carmody.'

'Jean Carmody?'

'No, sorry, my mistake. I'm Emma Carmody, Jean's sister.' Her eyes narrowed suspiciously. 'You're not a reporter, are you?'

'Oh, no,' said Kitty earnestly. 'My grandmother was a very dear friend of Miss Watcombe. I've just come to pay my respects.'

Emma Carmody looked the stranger up and down. She certainly seemed like a respectable young lady, well dressed and extremely well spoken.

'My sister's quite tired,' she said. 'It's only ten minutes since the police were here.'

Kitty looked crestfallen. 'I've come quite a long way on the bus, do you think she'd be happy to see me, just for a few minutes? It would have meant such a lot to my grandmother. Miss Watcombe always spoke so highly of your sister.'

Emma's face relaxed. She definitely didn't seem like a reporter. Far too refined and well-spoken.

'I'm sorry Miss. I suppose I'm just being overcautious. We had two separate reporters here yesterday. One of them put his foot in the door. How rude! Good job I had my mop, he didn't seem quite so insistent after I'd hit him on the shins.'

'I can assure you I am definitely not a reporter,' Kitty said with her most winning smile.

'Of course, please do come in.'

She held the door open and Kitty stepped inside. The house was very small but spotless, a long hallway with doors off and a steep staircase to one side.

'Can I tell her who's calling?'

'Yes, sorry, of course. Miss Archibald. Miss Alice Archibald.'

'She's resting but I'll let her know you're here. Would you mind waiting?'

Emma Carmody disappeared through the door at the far end of the hall, returning moments later.

'She'd be very happy to see you Miss Archibald. Here, let me take those flowers from you. I'll put them in a vase for Jean. Would you like some tea?'

'Yes please, that would be lovely.'

'Of course. Please, go on through.'

Jean Carmody looked up from her seat on a small sofa in the back sitting room as Kitty entered.

Kitty took in a shallow breath.

She wasn't sure she had ever seen a woman as beautiful as Jean Carmody in her entire life.

Kitty thought Jean was in her late thirties. Her hair was a startling shade of white blonde, fashioned into a stylish marcel wave. Her features were fine and delicate, her skin like the most perfect translucent porcelain and her eyes were the colour of wild cornflowers in an English meadow. Her full lips were bright red, expertly and beautifully painted.

She certainly did not look like the common painted harlot Mrs Lockhart had alluded to. Kitty wondered idly if, in Lockie's book, being an extremely attractive and obviously desirable woman who also happened to be in service was somehow a sin in itself.

Jean Carmody stood up and held out her hand, the fingernails short and as blood red as her lips.

'Miss Archibald, how lovely of you to come.'

Kitty shook her hand. 'It's lovely to meet you Miss Carmody but I'm sorry it's under such sad circumstances.'

Now she was closer, Kitty could see her eyes were slightly red-rimmed and there was a delicate red blush on the tip of her perfect nose, as if it had not been long since she had been crying. Kitty could see a handkerchief almost concealed in one hand.

'Thank you, that's very kind of you to say. Please, take a seat.'

Emma Carmody came into the room with a large tea tray, the carnations, which were now in a vase, precariously balanced on one end, the teapot on the other.

'Oh, how beautiful. Thank you,' said Jean, seeing the flowers. 'That was so thoughtful of you.'

'My sister says your grandmother was a friend of Miss Watcombe?'

'Yes, I believe they met in London. I know they remained friends for many years before my grandmother passed away just before the war started.'

'What was her name?'

'Millicent Archibald.'

'I don't recognise the name, but then Miss Watcombe did have a lot of acquaintances, especially when she was young.

'Well, it's just nice of you to come anyway, and so nice to see a friendly face,' said Jean Carmody, sipping her tea. 'I'm afraid after what happened, and now with William being arrested, I'll not see many more of those in the future.'

Take the bull by the horns, Kitty said to herself.

'Yes, I'm so sorry about that. It must have been a terrible shock. My grandmother said Miss Watcombe was a kind lady so it's just awful what happened to her. And I am so sorry about your brother.'

'Half-brother,' Jean corrected. 'Emma and I were already quite grown up when our father died and our mother married Bill and then had William. Bill was a rough sort by all accounts.' She stared into the distance for a moment, her eyes unfocused.

'And don't they say the apple never falls far from the tree?' she added, looking back at Kitty.

Her eyes started to tear up and she dabbed at them with her handkerchief, but her expression was steely and oddly defiant.

'I know everyone says he did it. I'm not making excuses for him, believe me, I know he's had a difficult time over the years but I know he would never do such a thing. Yes, he liked to take things that didn't belong to him, and he's paid the price for that, but I've never seen our William lift a finger against anyone, not a man or boy, and most certainly not an old, frail woman. I don't care what people are saying, I will never believe that he did it until the day I die.'

'Well, I don't know whether it's true, but I did hear they had a lot of evidence against him.'

Jean Carmody scoffed, taking another sip of tea to steady herself.

'Yes, I heard that too. A bloody knife on his person

apparently, and something about a silver plate under his bed. William is many things but he isn't stupid. Why would he hide a knife where anyone could find it? And, as for the plate, that makes no sense either. Lord knows how he got his hands on it in the first place and he swore to me he was leaving his life of crime behind once and for all. He was so grateful to Miss Watcombe for giving him a second chance and I know he wouldn't have done anything to jeopardise the opportunity she'd given him.'

'What about her pearls? I heard Miss Watcombe had some beautiful pearls that are missing. Is it likely William stole them sometime beforehand and hid them away?'

'Impossible,' Jean Carmody responded passionately. 'Miss Watcombe never took her pearls off, except when she went to bed and she always laid them out on a velvet pouch on her dressing table. I used to say to her, Miss Watcombe, you should buy a safe or let me put them somewhere more secure but she wouldn't hear of it.

'I know it's hard to believe when someone is old and frail, but when she was young, Miss Watcombe was a renowned beauty. Her father was a very senior official in the Governor's office, in Bengal or Simla, I forget which. It was rumoured that she was even pursued by Prince Albert when he visited India. He wanted Miss Watcombe to become his mistress but she'd hear none of it, of course.

'Men would just fall at her feet wherever she went. She said the Mannar pearls had been given to her by a young Maharaja who was hopelessly in love with her, and she never let them out of her sight.'

'So, if you're convinced William didn't do, who do you think did?'

Jean sighed, suddenly looking deflated. 'I don't know. We didn't have many visitors to the house, not in recent years, and Miss Watcombe was quite easily the kindest, most wonderful, gentlest soul who ever lived.'

She dabbed at her eyes again. 'Why would anyone want to do anything so evil?'

There was a moment's silence as if Jean Carmody was reflecting on a true friendship, cruelly taken away.

Kitty was itching to ask her more but stopped herself. If she wasn't careful, this would start sounding like an interrogation and not just one kindly, and completely disinterested party, offering condolences to someone who had obviously lost a person very dear to them.

Kitty glanced at her watch. She had been here for about twenty minutes and she thought Jimmy might be getting restless by now.

She stood up to leave, and Jean Carmody stood up as well.

'Thank you for seeing me. I know you must be very tired so I didn't want to keep you too long. I just want to say again I am so sorry for your loss.'

They shook hands but Jean suddenly looked quizzical.

'My sister said you'd come today because Miss Watcombe spoke kindly of me, but didn't you say your grandmother died before the war? I didn't join Miss Watcombe until 1915.'

Kitty swallowed down a slight bubble of panic. Detail, she chided herself, detail.

'Sorry, did I say the *before* the war? Silly me, I do get so muddled sometimes. I meant after the war. Actually in 1919. They hadn't met in person for a very long time, but I believe they still corresponded until then and Miss

Watcombe told my grandmother what a wonderful support you were to her.'

Jean Carmody's face relaxed.

'Oh yes, that makes sense now. I very rarely saw Miss Watcombe's outgoing post so it's not surprising I didn't recognise your grandmother's name. Miss Watcombe was very active and bright minded until the very end. Up until December, she used to go into town every Thursday morning, regular as clockwork, to go to the bank, have her hair set and post out her own correspondence too. Frank Fogwill, the landlord at The Ketch Inn, used to drive her in and wait for her, which was very kind of him.'

She thought again.

'And so lucky you were able to find me here?'

'Well, I have to admit, I'm a bit of an amateur sleuth,' said Kitty, thinking fast. 'My grandmother said Miss Watcombe had told her you had family in Brixham, so I just looked up Carmody in the phone book. I think your sister was the only one so I took a chance. I was just glad your name isn't Smith or Jones.'

Despite the circumstances, Jean let out a small laugh.

'How clever of you. Yes, you're right. Emma is the only Carmody in Brixham and I'm very glad you did. It's been a pleasure to meet you Miss Archibald.'

Jean walked Kitty to the door, saying their goodbyes, and Kitty walked back to the car on legs that felt decidedly more wobbly than she would admit to Jimmy.

He was standing next to Betty when she turned the corner, having obviously decided that he might actually seize up completely if he spent any longer squashed into the small car than was absolutely necessary.

He looked relieved to see Kitty. 'How did it go?' he asked as they both got back in to the car. Kitty let out a big puff of breath. 'Interesting,' she said. 'A couple of hairy moments, but I think I got away with it.'

Jimmy looked at his watch. 'Listen, I've got to get back and type up these notes. Shall we meet up later to discuss what we've learned?'

'Good idea,' said Kitty, starting the car. 'Nora and I are helping at the church fete so why don't you come over on Sunday afternoon for tennis, if you're not on duty? That'll give us time to think things over.'

'Will do, and I'm going to the inquest tomorrow so I'll be able to tell you all about it on Sunday.'

They drove back to Torquay in silence, each lost in their own thoughts about their conversations with Jean Carmody.

8

A break-in at the scene

Laburnum Villas stood on a corner and had once, many years before, been two houses but was now a single substantial property with white rendered walls, a steep slate roof and tall chimneys. When John and Caroline Markham had bought both houses, it had been ideal. With some new walls erected, some walls dismantled, and a few additional doors added here and there, the smaller property made a perfect separate annex for John's surgery, with a small waiting room, consulting room and study. With some rearrangement of the garden walls, the main house was private and accessed via Brunel Close while the surgery was separately accessed via Combe Manor Road.

Glencoe, which fronted wholly onto Combe Manor Road was, in truth, a much more grand house than Laburnum Villas. It was older, a Gentleman's residence in design, solidly built of brick with a lovely symmetry that the slightly higgledy-piggledy Laburnum Villas lacked. The central front door was imposingly grand, protected by a porch with fluted columns and a copper roof, and flanked by regular banks of long casement windows on either side.

What Laburnum Villas and Glencoe did have in common was extensive lawns and shrubbery, the back gardens of the properties divided one from the other by an old, tall, brick wall.

At the farthest end of the garden, hidden behind a large skimmia on the Markham's side and an equally impressive euonymus on the Glencoe side, a few of the old bricks at the base of the wall had decayed over the century since they'd been laid and broken away, creating a hole between the properties of about six inches across by ten inches deep.

When Arthur and his mother had come to Glencoe, he was nearly six and the twins eleven. Arthur's mother had been overly protective of him and had tried to discourage him from mixing with the Markham girls. She felt they were too headstrong for her delicate son, so the three had had to resort to sending silly notes to each other through the hole in the wall.

When they noticed that some of the notes were ending up wet and unreadable, Nora asked Mrs Lockhart for an old biscuit barrel which they placed in the hole, equidistant between each side. It was their secret, a hidden message system known only to Kitty, Nora and Arthur. It came in particularly handy now when they wanted to communicate with Arthur but didn't fancy facing the wrath of Miss Davey at the front door, or when Arthur had been confined to the house and gardens after another damning end-of-term report from Charlton School.

After tea, with his father already gone out to a Lodge meeting and Miss Davey settled down in front of the wireless with her knitting, Arthur excused himself on the pretence of going into the garden to hit a few cricket balls while it was still light.

'Not near the house Arthur,' Miss Davey shouted as he let himself out of the back door.

Unseen, he ran to the bottom of the garden and side-shuffled around the euonymus, reaching inside the hole to extricate the biscuit barrel. It had grown rusty over the years, but the lid still shut firmly, and he prised it open and took out a piece of blue writing paper, folded into quarters. Without looking at it, he tucked it firmly into his trouser pocket, closed the lid and put the tin back inside the wall.

Time to look at it later in the privacy of his bedroom, he thought.

Now, a few cover drives and full tosses before he had to go in.

*

As the light faded completely and night fell, Arthur excused himself from the parlour, telling Miss Davey he fancied reading in his room.

With the door firmly shut, Arthur unfolded the piece of paper he had taken out of the biscuit barrel earlier and read through it.

Miss Eleanora Markham
Laburnum Villas
Wellesmead
Torquay

Arthur
If you can, go to Rockcliffe House, either
tonight or tomorrow after dark and see if
you can find anything interesting. Take a
torch and make sure you aren't seen.
Come over for tennis and a debrief on
Sunday at two o'clock,
Nora

p.s., Ask Sir Charles to call Dr Markham if
you need permission (for the tennis obviously,
not the breaking and entering).

Arthur liked Nora. He liked Kitty too, of course, but
there was something no-nonsense about Nora that appealed
to him. Kitty was more theatrical but Nora didn't bother to
sugar-coat anything. She was straight up and down. Hadn't
she been the one who said he might well fall to his death
when he'd shimmied up that tree to retrieve Horus? He liked
that. Direct and to the point.

Arthur lay on his bed for an hour or so reading. While
he did occasionally read the detective novels that Kitty, Nora
and Jimmy liked, Arthur much preferred daring tales of
spies and espionage, shadowy figures in foreign wars, lies

and guns, deceit and bombs. He picked up his copy of 'The Three Hostages' and found his place.

He thought he might have dozed off for a while but, when the hall clock chimed midnight, he woke up with a start. His book had slid to the floor and he picked it up and put it on his nightstand.

He got up and put on a pair of black trousers and a black jumper over a dark blue shirt. He added his black plimsolls, then lifted up the sash window and peered outside into the still, summer night. After a clear day, a few clouds had bubbled up and drifted lazily across the moon, offering moments of useful darkness.

All was preternaturally quiet.

Arthur tucked his small Scouts torch inside his jumper and, sitting on the windowsill, swung his legs over the edge. His toes touched the wisteria and he tentatively leant forward and grabbed a thick part of the twisted stems.

It was not the first time Arthur had climbed out of his window.

One Sunday last year, he had been in the garden, bouncing his cricket ball up and down on his bat before deciding to try for a cover drive. The ball duly flew off with alarming speed in an uncontrolled direction and promptly smashed through the greenhouse window. Sir Charles had sent him to his room for the rest of the day and, out of boredom, Arthur had decided to see if he could climb down the wisteria and spent a happy few hours going down, and back up again, totally unseen.

He wiggled his right foot into a secure, comfortable position and manoeuvred himself fully outside. The wisteria groaned a little under his weight but held firm.

Swinging down, methodically and steadily, foot over

foot, hand over hand, Arthur reached ground level and dropped silently down onto the lawn.

He waited as a large cloud temporarily blocked out the moonlight and then ran, hunched over, for the gate, closing it quietly behind him and setting off down the road. Walking fast, he hugged the line of the hedges and garden walls until he got to the main road.

Wellesmead at that time of night was largely deserted. A single car went by and two men who were walking on the same side of the road as him, smoking and talking quietly, crossed over as he approached.

Arthur decided he liked being out at this time of night. He wondered that, if he didn't fulfil his dream of playing cricket for England, whether he should consider a career as a gentleman cat burglar?

He slipped unseen past the funicular carriage, locked and silent at the top station and made his way quickly down the path towards the sea, turning right at the bottom as the three friends had done the day before.

The clouds seemed less here, and the moonlight was quite bright, but he still watched his feet carefully. It would be awfully hard to explain if he tripped over a bramble and broke his ankle.

He slowed as he reached Rockcliffe House. The little shingle beach was empty, the only signs of any life a few lights shining from the windows of the inn and the soft glow of lamp light from a couple of the fishermen's cottages. Everything else was silent and deserted.

He stopped and his heart missed a beat.

There was a policeman outside the house in almost the exact same place that Jimmy had been standing. As Arthur stared, he realised the man wasn't moving. He appeared to be leaning back against the wall, his eyes closed and his chin low on his chest.

Arthur listened carefully. Was that snoring? He thought it was, and he smiled. Perfect.

Slipping quietly over the low wall between the ironwork pillars that held up the veranda, Arthur crept around the house until he was at the farthest point away from where the officer was slumbering.

This end of the house had been less affected by the fire, and he found the door that led to the scullery unlocked. As he stepped inside, he wondered if he got caught, could he rightly claim that technically he was just entering, and not breaking and entering?

Inside it was very dark and the dank, musty smell similar to that of a bonfire extinguished by a heavy shower assaulted his nostrils. He turned on his little torch but shielded the beam so it only cast a low light on the floor in front of him. He walked slowly from room to room, trying to get his bearings. Through an inner hall, a side pantry and a neat kitchen, largely unaffected by the flames, before he found a short staircase with a door at the top. He emerged out into the main hallway.

Here was the first real evidence of the devastation the fire had caused. What had been a white painted staircase was almost completely burned away at the bottom, the remaining paint curled and peeling from the heat. The parquet floor was starting to lift in places ruined by the water, and there was an acrid lingering smell of smoke that seemed to pervade the very fabric of the building.

To one side of the hallway, the fire had obviously been

at its most fierce, the wallpaper completely blackened, the timbers buckled and the central chandelier hanging precariously by a few wires, most of the crystals having shattered under the ferocity of the heat.

Arthur suddenly felt apprehensive. He had never been at the scene of a murder before and he could not ignore the sound of blood as it rushed in his ears.

He hesitated just inside the doorway of the sitting room, surveying the scene. A large Chinese rug that covered most of the floor was dirty with ash and fallen timbers but, as Arthur played his torch beam across the floor, he couldn't help seeing an irregular shape in the centre of the carpet that showed bright reds and greens as the light played across it. Large black stains covered parts of the floor and walls, the yellow honeysuckle flowers on the wallpaper spattered and soiled.

He swallowed hard. He didn't need anyone to tell him that this is where Miss Watcombe's lifeless body had lain, protecting the carpet against the ravages of the fire.

Arthur looked away, trying to ignore a rolling queasiness in his stomach.

There was a heavy bureau to one side of the room which was open, and a cascade of papers had drifted down and littered the floor, some burned to ash, others just singed around the edges, some lying in soggy clumps. He gently leafed through a few sheets that still clung to the writing plane, but nothing of note caught his eye. A few receipts, a letter from the haberdasher telling Miss Watcombe that the bolt of fabric she had ordered had arrived, a card from her dentist detailing the date and time of her next appointment.

Arthur was not the sort of young man who frightened easily, but he suddenly felt the presence of Miss Watcombe all around him. Kindly but distraught, trying to tell him something. A feeling, both comforting and terrifying, permeated the broken house.

He heard a sound outside, heavy footsteps walking along the pavement at the front of the house.

Time to leave.

Lowering his torch as much as he could, Arthur started to retreat and the beam of light glinted across something shiny on the floor, lying beside the leg of a small armchair.

A thick, unpleasant rivulet of dark material stained the upholstery and had dripped down, pooling on the floor.

There it was again. Something small and shiny. Swallowing down the taste of bile that rose up in the back of his throat, Arthur reached down, ignoring the feeling of his fingertips on the sticky residue.

He put the edge of the object between his thumb and forefinger and pulled it up. It resisted for a moment, but then came free.

It was a small piece of metal in the shape of a flattened semi-circle with tiny holes at the top and bottom.

Not stopping to inspect it more closely, Arthur wrapped it in his handkerchief and stuffed it unceremoniously into his pocket.

The footsteps outside were getting louder and then stopped. Turning off the torch, Arthur deftly retraced his steps, quietly shutting the door to the downstairs kitchen, and letting himself out the way he had entered through the scullery door.

As Arthur climbed over the wall, he saw the back of the policeman walking in the opposite direction, no more than ten yards from him.

Arthur walked as fast as he could until he reached the sanctuary of the shadows at the head of the path, and then ran without looking back.

He was not sure he breathed again until he had scaled the wisteria, clambered in and shut the window behind him, overwhelmingly grateful to be standing back in the peace and security of his room.

Arthur would never tell a living soul but he was convinced he had felt the hand of Miss Watcombe's murderer reaching out for him, the killer's cold breath on the back of his neck, all the way home.

9

Antwerp September 1917

TELEGRAM...TELEGRAM...TELEGRAM...TELEGRAM
Antwerp September 18th, 1917

Mlle M. STOP The bird cage will be open for two hours at 0800 Tuesday next while the cat is occupied with a mouse. Intercept the canaries and transport to the location agreed STOP Await further instructions on how and when to release them back into the wild. Destroy this note STOP Good luck STOP Alfonse

TELEGRAM...TELEGRAM...TELEGRAM...TELEGRAM
Antwerp September 24th, 1917

Alfonse STOP The release has been compromised STOP Have retreated safely but the canaries have been discovered and executed at the scene STOP Secure sources advise extreme caution in our dealings with high command. My heart is broken that we are not all on the same side STOP trust no-one STOP Mlle M.

10

Anyone for tennis?

Sunday dawned fair and clear, the azure blue sky flawless and the air already warm. It promised to be the hottest day of the summer so far and perfect for a tennis party.

After lunch, Mrs Lockhart caught the bus to Paignton to visit her sister Violet, Jimmy's grandmother, and John Markham had wasted no time getting out to his garage. With the doors open, a gentle breeze playing around his feet and cricket on the wireless, he was perfectly happy, lovingly sponging Betty down after her drive the day before.

Kitty, Nora and Arthur were already on the tennis court, waiting for Jimmy.

Sunday was a good day for tennis.

Kitty and Nora's father had decided it was not economic to have a full-time gardener anymore but Willie Hockings came over each Saturday through the summer to clip the hedges, deadhead the roses and mow the lawns and the grass court.

Willie had been the head gardener over at Stanford Hall until reluctantly he had to admit his knees and back could no longer take the bending, stretching, kneeling and sheer physical toll that working full time in such a large garden had on his body. He had moved with his wife Edith to a small modern bungalow in town, with a perfectly pleasant postage stamp of lawn and a few assorted tubs that Edith liked to grow pansies in. He was delighted, after three months of his enforced retirement, that he had bumped into John Markham in the Post Office.

They had got talking, and Willie's eyes had lit up when Dr Markham started to complain about the state of his shrubbery. Willie offered his services, at a very reasonable rate, to work at Laburnum Villas one day a week. It got him out of the house for a few hours and some much welcomed beer money. Better than that, his joints could easily cope working one day on, six days off.

That Sunday, the tennis court was looking pristine. Not only had Willie mown the lawn the day before, he had also rechalked the lines and tensioned the net which had a habit of sagging if left too long.

The three waved to Jimmy as he came down the path and cut across the lawn, his white flannels flapping in the breeze. He had a small duffle bag slung over one shoulder, the handle of his tennis racket sticking through the neck.

'Hello all,' he said, flopping down into one of the lawn chairs under a large umbrella, next to the twins and Arthur. It offered welcome shade on such a hot day and Jimmy took out his handkerchief and wiped some beads of sweat from his forehead. He had already worked up quite a glow on the walk uphill from the bus stop in the centre of town.

'Lemonade?' Nora asked, reaching for the jug and a spare glass before he had even had time to respond. 'Yes please,' he said anyway, taking the glass gratefully and almost draining it in one go. 'Gosh, I needed that,' he said with an appreciative sigh, wiping his mouth with his hand.

Not one for small talk, Nora put her own glass down. 'So, do we want to play first, or are we going to talk about what we've learned about the case and play later?'

'Let's have one set first,' said Kitty, standing up and picking up her racquet. 'I'll play with Jimmy. Nora, okay with Arthur?'

Arthur was small but Nora knew he had a solid game. What he lacked in terms of reach and stride length, he more than made up for with speed and agility, and a whippy, left-handed serve that often proved problematic for any opponent.

'Of course, we'll wipe the floor with you! Come on Arthur, let's have a knock-about first.'

They played a tight set, which Nora and Arthur won 6-4. The games had gone with serve until Arthur broke Jimmy, and then Nora went on to easily serve it out to love.

'That wasn't fair,' complained Jimmy good-naturedly, as they went to sit back down in the shade. 'I've just walked three miles to get here, most of it uphill, and I'm wearing long trousers!'

'Maybe you should buy some shorts like Arthur?' Nora joked.

'I don't think so,' replied Jimmy with a look of mock horror. 'All right for a boy but not for a man, Standards, Nora, standards.'

Kitty poured four glasses of now very warm lemonade, and they drank in silence for a moment.

'How was the inquest yesterday, Jimmy?'

'I can't believe we had to stay home and beat rugs with Lockie!' added Nora, still peeved.

'As expected, murder, no question. I expect there'll be a write up about it in tomorrow's paper.'

'Shall we take it in turns to share what we've learned?' said Arthur and the others nodded in agreement.

'Who wants to go first?'

Jimmy reached into his bag and took out his small black policeman's notebook. 'I suppose I should as I'm the only official person here.'

He flicked through the pages until he came to where he had started his interview with Jean Carmody two days before.

'I'll run through some of the basics quickly,' he said, licking his thumb and flicking forward a few pages. 'Jean Margaret Carmody, aged thirty-nine. Has worked for Miss Watcombe, primarily as a cook but also as a sort of housekeeper and companion, for just over fifteen years.'

He scanned down his notes.

'Her half-brother, William Neck, the accused. Twenty-two years of age. According to Jean, he's been in and out of prison since he was about fourteen, mostly acquisitive stuff. Theft from the person, shoplifting, house burglary. Never anything violent though. He was in prison this year until May when he came out after three months for stealing a watch and went to work for Miss Watcombe at the beginning of June.'

'Did she say how he'd come to be employed by Miss Watcombe?' asked Kitty.

'Jean said she must have been looking worried one day

and Miss Watcombe asked her what the matter was. Jean told her William was due out of prison any day and was looking for gainful employment. She'd apparently been trying to find him work but, not surprisingly, many people hadn't wanted anything to do with someone with a record like William's.'

'Doesn't it seem odd that Miss Watcombe would have offered him a job at the house? She could just have helped find him work somewhere else if she'd wanted to.'

Jimmy looked up from his notebook. 'Apparently not as odd as you might think. According to Jean, Miss Watcombe always had a thing about prisoner rehabilitation. Used to be one of her pet interests back in the day, along with the care of orphaned children and the welfare of working animals.

'She certainly seemed to love a lost cause,' he added.

'Did Jean say anything about how William reacted to getting his new job?'

He looked back at his notebook.

'She said he was really pleased. He wasn't one to show much emotion apparently, Jean thinks that sort of thing got beaten out of him in prison, but she could tell he was grateful. It wasn't much but he'd told his sister he was determined to turn his life away from crime and this was going to be the perfect opportunity.'

'Did you ask her about the pearls?'

'No, I forgot,' said Jimmy, looking disappointed that he had apparently forgotten something that might be so crucial. 'Don't worry,' interjected Kitty, 'I did. I'll tell you in a minute.'

Looking relieved, Jimmy read on.

'I asked her about the relationship between William and Miss Watcombe. Interestingly, she admitted they had

had a minor falling out two days before the murder. Miss Watcombe felt that there wasn't enough meaningful work for William to do at the house so was dropping his hours slightly which would have meant two shillings less in his weekly wage.'

'That could be enough of a motive,' said Arthur, and the others nodded in agreement.

'Yes, it could, but Jean stressed it hadn't been more than a few choice words from William on learning his wages were going to be cut, and that he apologised to Miss Watcombe later for his rudeness.'

'Was there anything else?'

'Not much,' said Jimmy, rifling through the remaining pages.

'I also asked her about Miss Watcombe's will. Jean said she definitely had one. She had shown it to Jean once, just the envelope it was in, not the document itself. She said she was letting her know where it was in case anything ever happened to her. Jean said it was kept in a locked drawer of her bureau in the Honeysuckle Room. Jean didn't know who the beneficiaries were, and Miss Watcombe never told her.

'She also said she wasn't sure who knew she'd be at her sister's that night. Miss Watcombe obviously, but she can't remember whether or not she specifically told William or the housemaid Nelly Crouch.

'Oh, and a couple of more bits of information from the station,' he added, closing his notebook. 'Nelly Crouch has made a statement confirming she saw William take the silver plate and hide it under his bed, and there were no fingerprints on the knife.'

They considered this in silence for a moment.

'Hmm,' reflected Kitty. 'Just because William stole the plate, doesn't necessarily mean he was the murderer though, does it?'

'Not necessarily,' agreed Jimmy, 'but it doesn't help his cause much either, especially as he's obviously lied about it. And you can bet the bank that the prosecution will have a field day. If he can lie about that, not much of an extra leap of imagination that he might lie about the murder too.'

Nora turned to Kitty. 'And what did you find out from your interrogation of Jean, Kitty?'

'Not much,' she sighed, 'and it was hardly an interrogation Nora. She was adamant that William wasn't capable of hurting anyone, let alone Miss Watcombe. And she was sceptical about the evidence of the bloody knife found in his overcoat pocket. She said there was no denying he was a criminal, but he wasn't by any stretch a stupid man, and that seemed like a very stupid thing to do.'

'What about the pearls?'

'Oh yes, the pearls. Interestingly, Jean said they'd been given to Miss Warcombe when she was a young woman in India and she never let them out of her sight. She wore them every day, and put them on her dresser by her bed at night. Seems pretty clear there was no way that William could have stolen them before the murder otherwise Miss Watcombe would have noticed and raised the alarm.

'She did say she couldn't think of anyone who might want to harm Miss Watcombe, but she admitted she wore her pearls into town, quite openly, so any number of people would have known about them. Jimmy, did she say anything to you about visitors to the house?'

Jimmy's eyes lit up slightly. 'Sorry, I forgot. I did ask her about that, and I asked her if she had any friends, particularly men friends, who ever came to the house. She's an extremely attractive woman, isn't she Kitty? Well, she said no, but I had a feeling she wasn't being totally truthful with me.'

'I liked her,' Kitty said simply. 'She seemed genuinely distressed about what had happened, but she was also totally convinced that William wasn't the murderer. I believe her.'

There was a pause.

'I believe her too,' said Jimmy.

Kitty, Nora and Arthur looked at him in surprise.

'I thought you were the one who was convinced it was an open and shut case? That there was only William in the frame?'

Jimmy nodded in agreement. 'I do, I mean I did, oh I'm not sure! My police head says he's guilty but, having met Jean Carmody and everything else we've learned, now I'm not so sure.'

'There do seem to be quite a lot of anomalies, don't there?' said Kitty, pouring herself some more lemonade.

'By all accounts, William was glad of his new job so why would he jeopardise that for a silver plate? He must have known that he'd be caught eventually and, when he was, he'd go back to prison for a very long time.'

'And he had never been violent before so it's quite a leap to think he'd gone from someone who would actively avoid confrontation, to someone who would bash in the head of a defenceless old lady, slit her throat and then try to set her and her house on fire.'

'And where are the pearls?' added Nora. 'We know that William can't have stolen them. If he did, he wouldn't have had time to hide them very well, and no one's found them yet. I agree with Jean. Why would someone who had been in and out of prison for most of his life, and knew the score, do anything so utterly imprudent as to put the murder weapon in his own pocket?'

They sat in silence for a moment, lost in thought.

Kitty looked up. 'Did you find anything at Rockcliffe House, Arthur?'

Jimmy looked up sharply as if to say, *what do you mean, did Arthur find anything at Rockcliffe House?* but she waved him shush before he could speak.

'Yes, I found this, but it's probably nothing. It just seemed a bit out of place,' Arthur replied, reaching into the back pocket of his shorts and taking out his handkerchief. The others lent forward to get a good look as he unfolded the layers of fabric.

'I wouldn't touch it, if I was you,' he said. 'I found it in a puddle of something dark and sticky.' He pulled a distasteful face. 'I think it was blood. I haven't cleaned it.'

He held up his hand, and they looked at the small metal object that Arthur had found, trying not to think too closely about the dark stains.

'Where did you find it?' asked Jimmy.

'On the edge of the rug, next to the bureau.'

'What is it?' said Kitty.

'Let me look Arthur,' said Nora, carefully taking the handkerchief from him and studying the object more closely.

'I think it's a heel plate. You know, one of those metal protectors that men have on their shoes to protect the leather soles.'

Kitty leaned in closer. 'Oh yes, I think you're right Nora. Father has something similar on his brogues.'

Nora fixed Arthur with a serious stare.

'Arthur, think carefully. Was this under the blood, in the blood, or on top of the blood?'

Arthur scrunched up his face, remembering the scene.

'It was sort of in and on the blood,' he replied. 'It was stuck to some blood underneath it, but there was also blood on top of it. I know that because, when I saw it, only one corner was sticking out. Look.'

He carefully turned the object over in his handkerchief and there was obviously dried blood on both sides.

'Why, is that important?' he asked.

'It could be,' said Nora slowly. 'If it was under the blood, so it was clean on the downward side, it could have been dropped before the murder. If it was bloody on the downward side, but clean on the top side, it could have been dropped after the murder. But if it had blood on both sides, doesn't that suggest it landed there as the murder was being committed?'

The three looked at her, a horrible thought swirling around that this tiny piece of metal was their first tangible clue, a silent witness to a heinous crime.

'Could it have come from one of the people at the scene, or one of the policemen?' asked Arthur.

'No,' said Kitty, picking up on Nora's logic. 'Then it would just have been bloody on one side.'

'Anyway, most policemen don't have those sort of metal guards on their boots, far too dainty,' said Jimmy.

Arthur carefully folded the corners of the handkerchief over the bloody metal shard and tucked it back in the pocket of his shorts.

'Was there anything else Arthur?'

'Not much,' he replied, picking at a scab that had dried on his knee. *Probably caught it on the wisteria* he thought. 'Did you say Jean Carmody said the bureau was always locked?'

'Yes. She said the key was kept in the lock but it was always turned shut. She said Miss Watcombe never left the bureau unlocked, not even for a moment, when she wasn't in the room. Why?'

'Well, it was open when I was there. There were papers scattered all over the place. Looked like someone had been going through them.' Jimmy gave Nora and Kitty a stare that said, *I'll speak to you later about letting Arthur snoop around at the scene of a murder.*

'So what do we do now?' asked Nora.

Kitty sighed. 'I don't know. We could show this new piece of evidence to Sir Charles. He might know what to do with it.'

Jimmy interjected. 'I think we should keep everything we've learned close to our chests for the time being. Everyone at the station thinks Neck's as guilty as sin, so I can't see them having any appetite for reconsidering the case, particularly with so little to go on.'

'I agree,' said Arthur. 'My father is like the cat that got the cream. You'd think he had solved this crime himself. He'd be a laughing stock if he reopened such a perfect case now.'

'I think there's only one thing for it then,' said Kitty.

'What?'

'Someone needs to speak to William Neck.'

Jimmy laughed, but stopped when he realised Kitty wasn't joking.

'Oh no, Kitty. Please don't say you should be the one to go to speak to him.'

Kitty looked mildly offended. 'Why ever not? They must be letting him have some visitors, the priest perhaps or his solicitor? I could pretend to be a friend, perhaps a lady friend if you know what I mean. Make them think I just want to say my final goodbyes before Sir Charles personally hauls him off to the gallows. If I could get five minutes with him, I think it would really help.'

Before Jimmy could disagree further, something caught their attention and they looked up to see Sir Charles striding around the side of the house and across the lawn towards them.

'Talk of the devil,' Nora whispered under her breath, and Kitty smiled.

Sir Charles was resplendent in white flannels and a white shirt, the sleeves rolled up and the collar open.

Despite age having deposited a few extra pounds around his midriff, Sir Charles was still a very active man, tall and athletic, if a little slower on his feet than he might have once been.

He had left the army after an illustrious war and joined the police force, rapidly rising up the senior officer ranks, as much for his ability to mix easily and confidently with the higher orders as for his policing skills. Despite the fact that he could be hard on Arthur, he was an affable neighbour, if a little old-fashioned in his outlook.

Jimmy quickly put his black notebook back into his bag and stood up.

'Good afternoon Sir, I mean Sir Charles, I mean Chief Constable,' he stuttered.

Sir Charles laughed, something he did on occasion although perhaps not as often as Arthur would have liked.

'Stand down lad,' he said in his soft Yorkshire burr, waving his hand up and down towards Jimmy. 'I'm not on duty and neither are you.'

'Hello, Sir Charles,' said Kitty, reaching for the jug. 'Would you like some lemonade? It's got a bit warm I'm afraid.'

'Not for me thank you Kitty. Perhaps later. Anyway, how's tennis going? I heard you were having a tournament.'

'Not so much a tournament, father,' replied Arthur. 'More a friendly knockabout.'

'Well, we'll have to see about that, won't we? Quite fancy a game myself. Has anyone got a spare racquet?'

'Here, Sir Charles,' said Jimmy, handing his over. 'If you four want to play, I'm happy to umpire.'

'Excellent. Arthur, you're with me. Let's see if the Westacott boys can best the Markham girls over three sets.'

He picked up one of the tennis balls and started to bounce it up and down on Jimmy's racquet, getting a feel for the strings.

'Oh, Nora, Kitty, before I forget. Is John around today?'

'I took Betty out for a drive yesterday so I imagine he's in the garage, picking the insects off her with a pair of tweezers!' Kitty joked.

'Ah, well, I won't disturb him. Can you just say there's an invitation to dinner at Glencoe on Friday for you girls and your father. Miss Davey has some new recipe she wants to try out on a few unsuspecting souls, Lord help us, and I didn't see why I should be the only one to suffer.'

'That would be lovely, thank you Sir Charles. I'll let father know when we go in.'

'Good, I'll let Miss Davey know as well so she can get her cauldron out. Right, let's spin the racquet for serve.'

*

In the end, the Markhams were no match for the Westacotts, losing 6:2, 6:2. What Kitty and Nora made up for in style and elegance was easily overcome by Arthur's dogged nimbleness and Sir Charles's superior strength.

They shook hands sportingly at the net.

'Well played girls,' said Sir Charles, looking at his watch. 'Come on Arthur, almost time for tea. Don't forget to tell John about Friday evening. Eight o'clock.'

'I'll walk with you to the gate,' said Nora.

They waved their goodbyes, and the trio disappeared around the side of the house.

Kitty and Jimmy sat back down in silence. Without the distraction of the game, Jimmy looked instantly pensive and deep in thought, staring at his fingers as he twisted them together on his lap.

Kitty glanced at her watch.

Two minutes passed. In all the years Kitty had known Jimmy Keyse, she was sure she had never known him not smile for more than one minute, forty-five seconds. Kitty knew something was worrying him greatly.

She picked up her lawn chair and placed it squarely in front of Jimmy's, sitting down so their knees were touching. He looked up and she reached over and took his two hands in hers.

He smiled wanly. 'Are we doing the right thing Kitty?'

'I don't know Jimmy. But if we don't at least try, how can

we live with ourselves if an innocent man is executed and we didn't do anything to prevent it?'

'I don't want to lose my job Kitty.'

Kitty tried to put on a bright smile in return. She squeezed his hands.

Jimmy let out a long sigh.

'All right, but none of your madcap schemes. I know you, Kitty Markham, you love the dramatics but we need clear heads and a foolproof plan if we're going to pull this off.'

He looked up. 'Good, here comes Nora. She's the most sensible person I know. Let's put our heads together and think of a way you can speak with William Neck and I'm not jobless by the weekend.'

II

The verdict is in

Wellesmead and Barnswood Examiner
Monday 28th July 1930

TORQUAY – Murder by person or persons unknown.

An inquest was held on Saturday 26th July 1930 at The Wellesmead Community Hall in the presence of Sir Albert Moxhay QC DFC, Coroner for the County of Devonshire.

Given the gravity of the offence, and the public interest, Sir Charles Westacott, Chief Constable of Devonshire, thanked the Coroner and the Jury for agreeing to convene on a Saturday.

The facts of the case being as stated below:

On Thursday 24th July 1930, the body of Miss Agnes Watcombe aged 73 was discovered at her home, Rockcliffe House, Smugglers' Cove Road, Wellesmead in the town of Torquay.

Dr David Arbuthnot of Marchhaven arrived at the scene at 2.45 a.m. at which time he was able to confirm life extinct. In his estimation, death occurred sometime after midnight which concurs with the discovery of a fire at Rockcliffe House at approximately 1.15 a.m.

In his initial assessment, Dr Arbuthnot concluded that the victim had died of exsanguination, consistent with a large gash on the left side of her throat and the quantity of blood at the scene. There was also some evidence of head trauma but this was not thought to be fatal.

Dr Arbuthnot also observed that the body had been partially burned, with severe charring on the left leg, left lower torso and right hand. Given the scene and injuries, Dr Arbuthnot concluded that death was not by natural causes or accident, but wholly consistent with a deliberate act perpetrated against the victim.

Additional witnesses interviewed:

Nelly Crouch, housemaid to Miss Watcombe

Miss Crouch was the first to discover the fire having smelt smoke from her room. She observed flames in the main hallway, stairwell, dining room and sitting room, known at the house as the Honeysuckle Room. Miss Crouch made her escape via the scullery door. She said a number of fishermen had already arrived at the scene and were assembling themselves into a line with buckets to bring water up from the sea. Miss Crouch said she ran to The Ketch Inn and woke up the landlord, Mr Francis Fogwill, who also attended the scene at some haste.

Francis Fogwill

Mr Fogwill confirmed he was awoken by Nelly Crouch, observing the time as he exited The Ketch Inn to be 1.24 a.m., albeit he did admit that his clock can sometimes run slightly fast. He attended the scene and, along with another man, fetched the water pump which was housed in the old Excise Boatman's cabin and proceeded to attempt to extinguish the flames. He instructed his potboy Jacob Garton to summon the fire brigade which Garton duly did, arriving shortly thereafter, accompanied by the police.

Jean Carmody, Cook and Housekeeper to Miss Watcombe

Miss Carmody attended the inquest but was not able to provide any material evidence of the crime, being away from home on the evening and night of the tragedy. She was, however, able to provide some insight into the character of Miss Watcombe as a gentle, generous woman who was known for her philanthropic works and kindness of spirit, particularly in relation to people less fortunate than herself.

Sergeant Fred Temple

Sergeant Temple said he was the first police officer on the scene, having arrived simultaneously with the fire engine. As the fire was extinguished, he proceeded to take oral statements from nearby witnesses. At some point, he was approached by Francis Fogwill who advised him that the owner of the house, Miss Watcombe, was not among the assembled onlookers. As soon as it was safe to do so, Sergeant Temple said that he, along with Francis Fogwill, William Neck and Edward Keane, entered the building and discovered the body of Miss Watcombe in the Honeysuckle Room. He confirmed they had tried to move the body, hoping to find signs of life but, on discovery that she was deceased, had exited the room and further help was summoned, including Dr Arbuthnot who arrived sometime soon after.

In conclusion, the jury had no hesitation in returning a verdict of Murder by Person or Persons Unknown.

In his summing up, Sir Albert Moxhay QC DFC stated:

'Murder in our fair county is thankfully a rare occurrence but, notwithstanding that comforting fact, this is indeed a terrible tragedy and the most serious of crimes perpetrated against an elderly, helpless woman in her own home. It is my understanding that a person has already been arrested on suspicion of causing the death of Miss Watcombe and that a large amount of physical and circumstantial evidence points to a single perpetrator. While a motive for this heinous act has yet to be established, the police are confident that it primarily involved robbery and/or theft from the person.

'I shall be making my full report available to the investigation and hope that the guilty party will suffer the consequences that justice demands, and as befits such a terrible and random act of unnecessary cruelty.'

12

The unexpected fiancée

The plan was all set for Tuesday afternoon.

Kitty and Nora sat at the dressing table in the bedroom they shared and went over the details again.

Jimmy said he would be walking his beat until about three o'clock when he would come back to the station to complete any paperwork before his shift ended at four.

He had checked the rotas and was pleased to see Sergeant Pell was on duty that afternoon. Jackie Pell was recently transferred from Durham and, by all accounts, was a fair and largely easy-going policeman.

Jimmy had said the timing was good as well. The middle of the afternoon was normally a quieter time at the station. Any criminals who favoured the night-time or early morning for their nefarious purposes had already been dealt with or had slipped away into the darkness unseen, and the evening criminals were mostly still lounging in bed, resting before their activities would commence.

Kitty was to loiter around outside the police station and await Jimmy's return.

'So, what look do you think we want to achieve?' asked Nora, opening the wardrobe and running her hands across the rack of dresses.

'Hmm, nothing too fancy but nothing too drab either. Plain and nondescript so that no one will be able to describe me after I've left.'

Nora held up a few items. 'No, too patterned. No, too bright. Definitely not the one with the turquoise parrots on it either,' remarked Kitty as each garment was rejected.

'How about this?' Nora asked, holding up a beige coloured light summer coat. 'Put this with a plain skirt. Oh, and this!' she added, picking up an old brown beret which had been discarded at the back of the wardrobe.

She tossed it to Kitty, who scraped back her distinctive dark bob and pulled the hat down low, tucking in a few straggly wisps until her hair was completely covered.

She picked up a paper tissue and wiped off her red lipstick until her lips were bare and then did the same with her cheeks, scrubbing away the rouge.

She felt butterflies in her stomach and turned back to look at her sister.

'Tell me you think this will work Nora?' she asked.

Nora considered the question for perhaps a second longer than Kitty would have liked.

'Of course it'll work. Simple. As long as you play your part, and Jimmy plays his, I don't see what could possibly go wrong.'

The sisters looked at each other and then burst out laughing, a nice release of the tension but perhaps tinged with a hint of hysteria.

'All right,' said Nora, taking control. 'Get changed and let's see what you look like. I'm just going downstairs to make sure papa and Lockie are otherwise engaged. They'd think you'd had a stroke if they saw you dressed in that awful hat and coat!'

Kitty quickly slipped into the plain skirt and blouse and then the coat, buttoning it up to the neck. She wished she could add a scarf but, given how warm it was, she thought that would have looked even more suspicious.

She was surveying herself in the mirror when Nora came back in.

'Will this do?'

'Perfect. Let's get going. No time like the present. Oh, and don't worry. Papa's in his study, I can hear the wireless and I can see Lockie from the window. She's outside picking cucumbers.'

'I'll walk with you to the end of Cedar Road if you like but then I'll see you back here later.'

Kitty took one last deep breath and looked at herself in the mirror. She was still pretty but perhaps less so in this drab garb and felt she would definitely pass muster as William Neck's lady friend.

They slipped out of the house and walked as quickly and quietly as they could towards Wellesmead's little shopping parade. By the butchers, they exchanged a brief hug and a whispered 'good luck' from Nora before she turned and headed back towards home.

Kitty started to walk towards the police station which was at the far end of the street, set a little way back and to one side of the last shop, Mr Jenning's news agency.

Kitty looked at the time. Two forty-nine. She walked

as slowly as she could, but not so slowly as to arouse any suspicion. The little row of shop windows offered endless opportunities to stop and linger unnoticed for a while. There was a nice green dress in Mrs Armitage's clothing emporium that Kitty stared at for a full minute and the banks of postcards in the Post Office, offering window cleaning services, pleas to find lost cats and details of flats to rent, offered her many minutes worth of loitering opportunity.

She looked up surreptitiously and was relieved when, at just a minute to three, she saw Jimmy turning the corner. He walked past Kitty without looking at her and headed towards the station.

She got into step behind him, and almost collided with him when he turned around at the station door.

'My goodness, Kitty,' he whispered in alarm. 'I didn't see you there.' He gave her a quick look up and down. 'And I certainly wouldn't have recognised you. You look ...,' he struggled to find the words, '.... you look so different.'

'Ready?' he asked.

'Ready as I'll ever be,' Kitty replied, and followed Jimmy into the police station.

Kitty had never been in a police station before. The little reception area was drably painted but bright, the summer light streaming in through two large windows. There was a tall counter with a policeman sitting behind it on a high stool, and a single bench of scarred wood along the side. At one end of the bench, an old man with an unshaven face and frayed clothes was sitting slumped against the wall, clearly asleep.

'Sit there please Miss,' Jimmy said with authority, and Kitty sat down at the opposite end from the vagrant.

Jimmy approached the desk.

'Afternoon Sarg,' he said and the policeman behind the counter looked up and smiled. He was about fifty, grey-haired and with a white moustache.

'Hello Constable Keyse,' he replied. 'Glad to see you back on time. No trouble in town?'

'No, nothing today. All quiet thank goodness. Anything to report here?'

'No. Gordon over there's a bit worse for wear as usual but he didn't want to go to a cell so I'm letting him sleep it off here.'

Sergeant Pell looked over towards Kitty and she lowered her eyes.

'Who's your lady friend?' he joked, winking at Jimmy.

'Very funny Sarg. Actually, I just bumped into her outside. She says she's a friend of William Neck. She asked if she could be allowed in to see him.'

Sergeant Pell shook his head. 'Not really the done thing, is it?' he said.

'Well, I know Sarg,' replied Jimmy. 'But have a heart. I heard he's off to Exeter next week and then, well, I can't see him getting back here after that. Or anywhere, in all likelihood, if you know what I mean?' He made a vague slicing motion on his neck.

Sergeant Pell laughed out loud, a deep throaty guffaw. 'Well, I think we'll be hanging him, not sending him to the guillotine, young James, but I know what you mean.'

He looked over at Kitty, not unkindly.

'I don't suppose it would matter for a few minutes. Young lady,' he said loudly, gesturing with his finger towards Kitty.

She stood up and approached the desk.

Sergeant Pell took a leather-bound ledger down off the

small bookshelf behind him. Kitty saw it said 'Visitors' in gold letters on the front.

'Name?'

'Dearlove, Edie Dearlove.'

Nora and Jimmy had told Kitty not to sound too educated or genteel but, luckily for them, Kitty was an excellent mimic and had spent enough time listening to Lockie to be able to deepen her voice and add a soft Devonshire burr, just authentically enough to be convincing.

'Relationship to the prisoner?'

'Fiancée, sir.'

Sergeant Pell laughed again as he wrote. 'Hope he knows that!' he joked.

He looked back at Kitty, his face now serious.

'You can have five minutes. Constable Keyse here will stay in the cell with you at all times so no funny business. No touching, no kissing, no passing notes to the prisoner and no accepting notes from the prisoner. And definitely no canoodling. Is that clear?'

Kitty nodded.

'All right, James, you can take her down.' He glanced at the clock. It was eight minutes passed three. 'Back by quarter past the hour, no later. Understood?'

'Understood.'

Jimmy turned to Kitty, taking the bunch of keys that Sergeant Pell handed to him. 'Come with me please Miss.'

Sergeant Pell lifted up the little hatched counter to the right of his desk, and Jimmy opened a door that led down a short corridor to some stairs.

As they made their way in silence down to the cells, the air became noticeably colder, the thick walls of the station basement offering little chance of the warmth or light of the summer day outside to permeate in.

Kitty's heart was beating so fast she thought Jimmy would be able to hear it, but he just led the way without looking back. She breathed in and out deeply, and it started to slow just a little.

They reached another door, locked this time. Jimmy cycled through the keys on the bunch he had been given and, finding the right one, unlocked it. They stepped inside and Jimmy pulled the door firmly behind them and relocked it.

Inside, the walls were painted black and the ceiling was low, their shoes echoing on the stone floor. There was a row of five doors on each side of a short corridor, each door with a small, barred opening at head height. A smell of stale cabbage and acrid male sweat assaulted Kitty's nose and she breathed through her mouth.

There was incoherent shouting from the nearest cell and Kitty could just see the outline of a man behind the opening. He was hitting the bars of his door with a metal plate.

'Quieten down, Ives,' shouted Jimmy as they passed the door and there was silence.

They reached the fourth door on the left and stopped.

'Wait here please Miss,' Jimmy said, not looking at Kitty.

He banged on the door of the cell.

'Neck, visitor for you,' Jimmy said, unlocking the door and not waiting for a reply.

Jimmy led the way into the cell and Kitty followed.

William Neck was sitting on the edge of a narrow, metal framed bed topped with a thin mattress and a rough blanket. To one side was a small table and chair, also metal and obviously of very poor quality and, in one corner, a bucket with a lid. There was no other furniture.

High on the far wall there was a window although, given how narrow it was, it should perhaps more accurately have been called an aperture. The glass was dirty and opaque and Kitty thought she could just see an inch of people's shoes as they walked along the street, oblivious to the watching eyes below them.

William Neck remained seated as Jimmy ushered Kitty into the room. He pushed the door closed but did not lock it, placing his back against the frame in case the prisoner decided he fancied his chances of an escape. Now, that would take some explaining.

'This young lady has come to see you Neck,' he said. 'She can have five minutes no more. No funny business, hear me?'

William stared at Kitty. Well, he thought idly, she was quite pretty but could probably make more of herself. What did it matter if a nice girl wanted to come and speak to him, at least it would pass five more minutes.

He motioned at the chair and Kitty sat down, facing him.

William Neck had a boyish face with regular features. He was not strictly handsome but his face had obviously inherited some natural symmetry from the Carmody side of the family and he wasn't unpleasant to look at. There was something about his eyes though that Kitty thought spoke of a hard life, a challenging upbringing and a path trodden that had not been kind to him. His eyes were round and fixed, and he stared at Kitty without blinking.

Kitty had never been this close to a real criminal before and she felt an urge to lower her gaze but resisted.

William looked away first.

'So, who are you and what do you want?'

Kitty looked back at Jimmy, who appeared completely

uninterested in the scene before him, studiously not paying attention to what was being said. She lowered her voice anyway as if to say, I don't want that policeman to hear.

'All you need to know is my name's Edie Dearlove and I'm your fiancée.'

William threw back his head and laughed.

Jimmy stared at him as William regained his composure.

'First off, love,' he whispered back, the sarcasm palpable, 'you don't look like an Edie Dearlove and second, and I can't stress this enough, I don't have a fiancée, so who are you and what do you want and if I don't get a straight answer, you can sling your hook.'

Kitty continued to stare back, reassured that it seemed to be making William Neck feel a bit uncomfortable.

She leaned in even closer, unintimidated.

'Listen, William. You don't need to know who I am. But apart from your sister Jean, I'm one of only a vanishingly small number of people in this world who don't think you killed Miss Watcombe.'

He flinched slightly. Good, thought Kitty, I think that touched a nerve.

'So what do you want?'

'Just the answers to a few questions. If you're honest with me, I am going to do whatever I can to get you out of here.'

'How, have you got a crowbar tucked under that awful coat?' he asked with a grin.

Kitty ignored him.

'Did you kill Miss Watcombe?'

'No I didn't.'

'Did you steal a silver plate from her and conceal it underneath your bed?'

'No I didn't.'

Kitty glanced over her shoulder again at Jimmy. He was now studying his fingernails.

'The police say they've got a witness who saw you take it and put it in your room.'

William shrugged. 'Well, they're lying. Who was it? Nelly Crouch? Listen, I wouldn't believe a word she says. Just as likely to be lying to protect that no-hoper of a boyfriend of hers, Eddie Keane. All I know is, I didn't take the plate, hear me.'

'Did you take Miss Watcombe's pearls?'

'Do I look stupid?'

'Is that a no then?'

'Of course it's a no. Granted, I can be a bit particular to the odd watch or bicycle but jewellery? Way out of my league I'm afraid.'

'Did you put the knife in your overcoat pocket?'

William stared at her for what felt like an eternity.

'Did you?' Kitty persisted.

'Yes, and I wrote 'It was William what did it' in poor Miss Watcombe's blood on the sitting room wall.'

Kitty's face was expressionless.

'I say again,' he repeated, picking a piece of lint off his trousers. 'Do I look stupid?'

'The police say you had blood on your trousers when you were arrested and kerosene on your boots.'

'More as likely my blood, I told them I cut my hand.' He held up his palm to show a nasty gash, just starting to scab over. 'Put it through the window when I found the fire. I thought it would help let the smoke out.'

'And the kerosene?'

'Wednesday was always my day for filling up the lamps

and those funny little heaters Miss Watcombe had. She said she felt the cold, even when it was so hot out. So, I could have spilled some then. I don't recall. Miss Watcombe would tell you that, if she were still alive.'

'But she's not, is she William?'

He suddenly looked a little uncertain behind the hard staring eyes.

'No she's not. But I didn't do it Miss, I swear.'

'Two minutes Miss,' Jimmy said from the doorway.

'I heard you had an argument with Miss Watcombe?'

William hesitated. 'We did have a few words. I suppose I'm not good at dealing with people yet, but I am trying. I told Jean and she said I'd acted wrongly. I went to apologise and Miss Watcombe was very kind. She was good to me, I would never have hurt her like they're saying.'

'William, can you think of anyone else who might have wanted to harm Miss Watcombe? Any visitors or suspicious looking people hanging about?'

William pursed his lips. 'Not that I remember. Mostly just the usual, you know, the butcher, the milkman, those sorts of people. Oh, and of course, Jean's man friend.'

Kitty jolted. 'What do you mean, Jean's man friend?'

'She had a fella, that's all I know. Used to come round once or twice a month.'

'Do you know who it was?'

'No, none of my business. I used to go out if I could hear them in her room, if you know what I mean. Jeanie deserved a bit of happiness. She's a kind person, too good for the likes of me. Anyway, that's all a bit irrelevant now, isn't it? Dare say I'll be out of her hair permanently in a few weeks.'

He looked up at Jimmy and raised his voice slightly. 'And good riddance to old rubbish, isn't that right, Constable?'

Jimmy didn't respond but tapped his watch in Kitty's direction. Hurry up, the gesture said.

'William, this is really important,' said Kitty, leaning in further. 'Is there anything else you can tell me about this man?'

'Not much. I never actually saw him. But I reckon he was a gentleman, or at least pretending to be one. He sometimes left his cane in the hall stand. Nice thing, dark wood, silver top. I saw it once when I was coming down the stairs. Had some sort of engraving of a bird on the end of it. Could have been a goose or a swan or perhaps a peacock.'

Jimmy coughed. 'Time's up, Miss. Let's be going.'

Kitty stood up. She reached into her coat pocket and took out a slip of paper which she folded and handed to William.

'Here's my name and telephone number. If you think of anything else, anything at all, ask the Sergeant to call me.'

Jimmy stepped aside and Kitty went to pass him, and then turned back to William.

'William, can I see the bottom of one of your shoes please?'

William lifted his leg and put his foot on the chair. Kitty could see a heavy leather work boot with a solid sole and dirt-encrusted hobnails.

'Do you own any other shoes?' she asked.

William laughed. 'Of course not, love. Who do you think I am, the King of Siam?!'

13

Seeing double

Following Nora's detailed instructions to the letter, Jimmy led Kitty in silence back to the front desk, saying a few words to the Sergeant and then turning around to start tidying up the notice board. Sergeant Pell signed Kitty out of the visitors book, and she left without a backward glance.

As she rounded the corner towards Laburnum Villas, Kitty took off the beret which was hot and making her scalp itch and she smoothed her hair into shape as much as she could. She nibbled her lower lip absentmindedly to bring some colour into it and pinched each cheek with the same aim.

She struggled out of the coat and undid the top two buttons of her blouse, relieved to feel some cool air on her skin. If she bumped into her father or Lockie before she got back to the safety of her room, she might strike them as somewhat overdressed for the weather but not so much that they would seriously start to question what she had been up to.

Thankfully unseen, she let herself into the house and quietly slipped up the stairs.

As arranged, Nora was already there waiting, lying on the chaise by the open window, her eyes closed and a copy of The Big Four on her lap.

She heard the latch and woke up almost instantly from her nap.

Kitty took off the blouse, conscious of how much it was sticking to her as a line of sweat trickled down her back. She stepped out of the skirt, balling both up and putting them at the back of the wardrobe. She would mix them in with some laundry when the weather had turned and when they wouldn't arouse any suspicion with Lockie.

Nora tossed Kitty her silk wrap.

'How did it go?'

'Marvellously all things considered. I got in and I got out, all in one piece and no one any the wiser I think. And Jimmy was absolutely magnificent. I'm tempted to see if he wants to join the Wellesmead Players with me next season.'

'So, you got to speak to William?'

'Yes, for about five minutes.'

'What was he like?'

Kitty sat down at the dressing table and applied some lipstick. *A woman really did not feel properly dressed without lipstick*, she thought.

'He acts like a little street urchin, like he couldn't give two hoots that he's in prison charged with murder. That in all likelihood he'll be sent to the gallows before the year's out. But I think under that hard shell, he's just a very scared young man.'

'Have you changed your opinion now you've met him? Do you think he did it?'

'I'm more convinced than ever that he didn't.'

'Did you learn anything new we can use then?'

'First of all, he said he didn't steal the plate. He was adamant, even though I told him the police have a witness to say he did. He guessed it was Nelly, but I said I didn't know. He mentioned she has a boyfriend called Eddie Keane. Said Eddie could just as easily have done it as him. Definitely one to look at, I'll ask Jimmy to do some digging about him.'

'Anything else?'

Feeling more human now she looked like herself again and not the mousy Edie Dearlove, Kitty turned around to look at her sister.

'Yes, something huge actually.' She paused for a moment.

'William said Jean has a man friend who came to the house.'

'No!'

'Yes, even though she told Jimmy specifically that she didn't and even told me that the household never had any visitors.'

'Did he know who it was?'

Kitty sighed. 'No unfortunately. He never actually saw him. He could just hear him and Jean together in her room. Oh, and he also said he thought he was quite well-to-do, or at least had aspirations in that regard. He said he had a nice cane with a bird carved on the silver top.'

Nora looked thoughtful.

'So what now?'

'I think it is probably a high-risk strategy, but I think we should go and see Jean, together. Tell her we know about the man who visited her at the house. Get her to come clean, even if it only means we can ultimately dismiss him from our investigations. Doesn't she at least owe that to William, a brother we know she loves and wants to help?'

Nora looked at her watch.

'Let's go into the garden. I left a message for Arthur to find a way to come over for a few minutes at four.' Kitty reached for a summer frock and got dressed as quickly as possible.

As they walked down the path to the bottom of the garden, a cricket ball came flying over the wall in front of them, accompanied by the sound of Arthur shouting 'Four!' from the next door garden, somewhat conflating his sports.

Five minutes later, Arthur appeared in the back garden of Laburnum Villas.

'Hello both,' he said nonchalantly. 'Miss Davey said I could pop round and retrieve my ball.'

'Hello Arthur. That was novel, but a bit close for comfort. Here it is,' said Nora, handing him back his ball with a wink.

'So, Kitty, what was he like? William. Was he frightening?'

'No Arthur, I'd say he was more frightened than frightening.'

'Did you learn anything new?'

'A couple of interesting things that Nora and I are going to look into further. We thought we'd take a drive over to see Jean tomorrow. Confess about the lie I told her about who I was and hope a bit of honesty persuades her to be equally honest.'

'About what?'

'We think Jean Carmody has a lover.'

Arthur looked a bit embarrassed at the thought of anything quite so unsavoury and could feel a rather hot blush blooming on his cheeks.

'And we need to find a man with a silver-topped cane

engraved with a bird,' added Nora. 'But that's probably going to be a dead end unless Jean confesses and we can link the cane to the man. Even papa's got one for special occasions, it's engraved with forget-me-knots. Our maman gave it to him the Christmas before she died.'

Arthur shrugged. 'My father has about six I think. He's got one with some sort of compass and set square design, another one with an elephant on it that some trophy hunter gave him in West Africa, and another one with some crumbling old ruin on it. No birds though.'

Nora laughed. 'I think you'll find the compass and set square are something to do with the Masons, and I've seen the one with the crumbling old ruin on it. I think it's Whitby Abbey, Arthur.'

'Anyway, there must be a thousand men in Torquay who have at least one silver-topped cane. Unless we stand on the corner of the High Street, looking at everyone that goes by, I don't think we can take that much further without a name to link it to.'

'And that heel plate definitely didn't come from William either,' added Kitty. 'I checked his boots.'

They stood in silence for a moment.

'I'd better be going,' said Arthur. 'I'm out of town tomorrow. Miss Davey is forcing me to go to Plymouth with her to get some new shoes ready for the start of term. My father didn't want the expense but Miss Davey said, if I didn't, she'd take her biggest pair of scissors and cut the toes out of my shoes and see how they liked that at school!'

'Leave me a note if you find out anything else,' he shouted back over his shoulder.

After Arthur had left, Kitty turned to Nora.

'Are you going to ask papa if we can borrow Betty again? I could pretend Myra Searle has taken a turn for the worse.'

'Who?'

'Never mind. Any ideas?'

'We could say we're going shopping?'

*

Kitty and Nora had come up with an elaborate story about Madame Roux's new autumn collection having just arrived and that they were dying to see what the latest styles were for the cooler weather but, in the end, the rouse was not needed.

Their father was singularly uninterested in his daughters' fashion needs and his only comment was in relation to Betty. 'What, twice in one week?' he said, just as the surgery telephone rang and he was suitably distracted.

'Good morning, Dr Markham speaking,' he said, listening intently as he rummaged around in the drawer for his pen. He waved vaguely in his daughters' direction.

Kitty and Nora left before he had time to finish his telephone call and ask the obvious question about why they were not going to Exeter on the train which would have been much more convenient.

The drive over to Brixham was uneventful, and Nora parked directly outside Emma Carmody's house.

They walked up the path in single file, Kitty rang the doorbell and they waited.

Moments later, the door was opened by Jean Carmody. She was looking as ethereal as Kitty remembered, her slim figure wrapped in a silk kimono, embroidered with red hummingbirds and blue hibiscus flowers. Her short blonde hair was immaculately waved and her eyes were still the colour of wild cornflowers, today brightened by the sunlight.

She looked at Kitty, and then at Nora, and then back at Kitty, a welcoming smile instantly dying on her lips. Her brow wrinkled into a furrow and a look of utter, stunned confusion spread across her fine features.

'Miss Archibald?' she said, again looking from one twin to the other, with an almost imperceptible shake of her head.

'Good morning, Miss Carmody,' said Kitty. 'I'm sorry, my name isn't Archibald I'm afraid. My name is Kitty Markham and this is my twin sister Nora. May we come in?'

Jean Carmody opened the door wider and stepped aside, obviously struggling with what to do or say next.

'Thank you,' said Nora, stepping into the narrow hallway. Kitty followed, giving Jean Carmody a reassuring smile as if to say I know how confusing this must be for you.

Jean indicated to the back of the house where Kitty had been before and the three women walked through into the small sitting room. Given its aspect at the back of the house and the dominance of the patterned sofa and armchairs it felt somewhat cramped.

They stood awkwardly in the small space.

'May we sit down?' asked Kitty.

Jean sat on the sofa and Kitty and Nora took the two armchairs opposite her.

'I know this must be very confusing for you. But I hope you'll let me explain,' said Kitty. 'My sister and I don't think William murdered Miss Watcombe. We think he's being framed but we have no idea why or by whom.'

'But who are you if you're not Miss Archibald? Did

you say your name was Markham? Are you related to Dr Markham over at Wellesmead?'

'Yes,' replied Nora, 'he's our father, but he isn't really relevant to why we're here. He doesn't know anything about it.'

'But I still don't understand. Why do you have any interest in helping my brother?'

Kitty hadn't really thought about it in those terms before. While Jean Carmody obviously had a degree of refinement well above her social position, her half-brother was not someone she or Nora would ever have associated with in the normal course of their lives.

A common criminal, socially low, angry, awkward, uneducated, coarse. But that didn't matter to Kitty, and she knew it didn't matter to Nora either, or Jimmy or Arthur.

She looked squarely at Jean Carmody.

'Because we believe he's innocent just like you do.'

Jean's eyes started to fill with tears, and she quickly reached for a handkerchief that she had in the voluminous pocket of her kimono. She dabbed at her eyes while she tried to compose herself.

'I'm sorry I deceived you when I pretended to be someone else. I thought I could get the information I needed without telling you the truth about who I was and why I was here, but I don't think that is possible. I think we need your help.'

'Of course, whatever I can do, just ask. Are you police women?'

Nora laughed, somewhat inappropriately given the circumstances, at the very notion. 'No, let's just say we're enthusiastic amateurs.'

Jean allowed herself a weak smile in return.

'Well, I don't care who you are or what you are, it's just wonderful to know someone else thinks it's inconceivable that William would have committed such a terrible crime.'

'I went to see William yesterday,' said Kitty.

'In jail?'

'Yes, in the cells at the police station.'

'How did you get in?'

'It's a bit of a long story. Let's just say we've got a friend on the force.'

'How was he? How was William when you saw him?'

'I think he looked remarkably well, given the situation he's in. Perhaps a little defensive and unhelpful, but I wasn't surprised by that. He doesn't know me and I think he's suspicious of anyone, apart from you, claiming to believe him.'

Nora glanced at Kitty. Let's cut to the chase, her look said.

'William told my sister that you have a lover who visits you at Rockcliffe House.' She held Jean's gaze until Jean looked down, her fingers knotting nervously in her lap.

'Yes, he's right. I did. I do. But I can assure you Miss Markham, Miss Markham, that he isn't in any way connected to what happened at the house that night.'

Kitty struggled to hide her exasperation. 'But why did you keep that information to yourself? Don't you see how crucial it could be to the defence in William's trial if there was possibly another person who could have been involved? Anything to put doubt of his guilt into the jurors' minds.'

Jean's expression hardened slightly. 'I'm well aware of that Miss Markham but it's a wholly moot point. My friend is in no way connected to this murder. You have my absolute guarantee on that.'

'I'm sure Mrs Crippen said the same thing,' Nora muttered under her breath, but not quite to herself, and Jean and Kitty both gave her a sharp look.

'So just tell us who he is so the police can speak to him and at least eliminate him from their enquiries,' implored Kitty.

'No.'

'Why not?' asked Nora, her tone more serious. 'Is he married?'

'I will never tell you and I will certainly not tell the police.'

'Well, we could just tell the police we know you have a lover you conveniently forgot to mention,' replied Nora, slightly coolly, studying her fingernails.

'Deny it to them if you want. I'm sure they won't be as understanding as we are if they think you've been obstructing their investigation by withholding crucial evidence.'

Jean stood up abruptly. 'I think I'd like you to leave now please.'

Kitty and Nora remained seated, Kitty throwing a harsh look in her sister's direction for good measure.

'Please Jean – can I call you Jean? Please Jean, sit down. Both of you, let's remember we are on the same side.'

Jean resumed her seat, narrowing her eyes at Nora and turning full on towards Kitty.

'Did Miss Watcombe know?'

'No. I didn't want to abuse her trust so we were very discreet.'

'Why are you so sure he's not involved Jean? And please, do call me Kitty.'

'Kitty, I just am. I like to think I'm an impeccable judge of character. I will just say he is a very respectable, law-abiding man, with absolutely no motive to do something so randomly cruel. Why would he? He isn't wealthy but he's not poor either and he certainly didn't have the opportunity. He would never have come to the house if he knew I was out and Miss Watcombe would never have answered the door anyway.'

'So he knew you were going to be away from home that night? Was it his suggestion?' asked Kitty.

'Absolutely not!' exclaimed Jean.

'He knew nothing about it until I told him. Emma has been having some health problems, women's trouble if you know what I mean, and I said I'd come over. Miss Watcombe suggested I stay the night as it's such a long way on the bus.

'My friend had actually said he might come over but I told him not to as I wasn't going to be at home. He was happy with that and we arranged to meet again the following week.

'I'm sorry I wasn't truthful but you need to put any thoughts aside that he might have been involved. He's a kind, gentle soul who is standing by me, which is more than can be said for many of my other friends and acquaintances.

'If you really want to help William, and I believe you do, you will need to find some other evidence to prove his innocence. I would hate for you to miss something while you're looking in completely the wrong direction for a connection that I can assure you does not exist.'

'I'm sorry if you thought I was harsh, Jean,' added Nora. 'But we're running out of time. We've been told William will be sent to Exeter sometime next week and we probably won't be able to do anything once the trial starts. You can trust us, you know?'

'I'm sorry too, but no. If I tell you, I know you will feel

compelled to tell someone, perhaps your friend in the police. Not out of maliciousness, but just because you think you're doing the right thing.

'But, do you know what will happen then? Whatever good reputation I have left, which I can guarantee is very little now most people think I'm the sister of a murderer, will have evaporated and what for? My chance of happiness will have gone forever, and none of it will have made a jot of difference to William's situation.

'Promise me you won't tell anyone?' she said, her gaze steady.

Kitty and Nora exchanged a glance. 'We promise, for now at least.'

'Thank you.'

'William also mentioned a man called Edward Keane, Nelly's boyfriend. Do you know him?'

Jean looked relieved that Kitty had changed the subject.

'Not well, I'm sorry. I think he's one of the fishermen who works out of the cove. William said he thought he remembered him from prison years ago when they were both much younger but he wasn't sure it was the same man.'

'We'll get someone to look into it,' said Nora, nodding slowly.

Kitty looked at her watch. 'We'd better be going soon. We told our father we'd be back by lunchtime at the very latest. Is there anything else, anything at all that you've remembered since I was last here?'

'There is one thing, although I'm sure its not important. I feel silly even mentioning it. Did I tell you when you were here that Frank Fogwill used to drive Miss Watcombe into town every week?'

'The publican? Yes, you did.'

'Well, she stopped going with him just before Christmas. She didn't say exactly what had happened but I got the distinct impression they'd had some sort of falling out over the house and garden.'

'Do you know what about? Did Miss Watcombe confide in you about what had happened?'

Jean shook her head. 'I don't really know but I think Frank was trying to persuade her to sell him the house and the land. Something about wanting to turn the house into a hotel or holiday accommodation, and tarmac over the garden to turn it into a car park. He used to say that now more people were getting motor vehicles they wouldn't want to walk down that steep road to the inn, and it would make sense to have somewhere for them to park, particularly given how tight the space is down by the cove, what with the sea on one side and the Rock on the other.'

'How did Miss Watcombe seem when she told you?'

'I think she was a little bit angry and hurt. I can't be sure but I think she felt like she'd been used by Frank, even taken for a fool. She couldn't abide insincerity and she was worried that Frank had just been nice to her to convince her that the house and gardens were too big for her now, and that she should consider selling up and moving into a retirement bungalow.'

Jean laughed. 'He didn't know it but he was wasting his time. That house meant everything to Miss Watcombe. There is no way she would have considered ever leaving it, and certainly not to see it pulled apart and her lovely garden destroyed.'

'Do you think he could be involved?'

'I don't think so,' answered Jean, looking perplexed by the notion.

'I went away for a week last year, just to Llandudno with Emma. I hadn't had a proper holiday in over five years and Miss Watcombe insisted. She was so thoughtful, she even gave me £5 as spending money.

'While I was gone, Frank's lovely wife Edna came over every day, regular as clockwork, with a stew, or some soup, or an apple pie for Miss Watcombe and to check she was all right and wasn't in need of anything.'

Jean looked wistful for a moment.

'Frank and Edna are such a loving couple, absolutely devoted to each other by all accounts, and always helping others less fortunate than themselves.'

'So you don't think the disagreement about the house could have pushed Frank into doing something rash? Perhaps he just meant to scare Miss Watcombe and things got out of hand?'

Jean shook her head. 'Honestly, I don't know, but I doubt it very much.'

'Did he know you were away from home that night?' asked Nora.

'I don't think so. There'd be no reason for him to have known.'

'And do you think Miss Watcombe would have let him in if you weren't there?'

'I very much doubt it. She liked Frank but, after they'd had words, I can't imagine her entertaining the thought of letting him in unannounced, unless perhaps Edna had been with him. The front door was always kept locked and bolted and I don't think she would have answered it anyway if she wasn't expecting someone.'

Kitty nodded at Nora and they both stood up.

'Thank you for your time Jean, and I am truly sorry for my deception last week.'

'Of course, and please don't apologise.' She turned to Nora, 'I'm sorry for being so rude earlier, as you can imagine this is a very stressful time.'

Nora smiled back. 'I'm sorry too.' She took a pen and slip of paper from her bag and wrote on it. 'Here, this is our telephone number, please call us if you think of anything else that might be helpful.'

'We'll be in touch,' added Kitty, taking Jean's hand and squeezing it tightly.

Back at the car, Nora looked at Kitty.

'We need to go and find Jimmy.'

14

Fancy a pint?

Sergeant Pell was doodling aimlessly on the blotter with his pencil. Trade was slow today. The odd drunk, someone asking the way to the train station, a lad who had stolen a loaf from the baker's and had been dragged into the police station by his mother. As was required, Sergeant Pell had given him a stern lecture about the evils of theft, a strategy that seemed to work as the eight-year-old left crying, promising never to commit such a horrible act of wanton criminality again.

He smelled her perfume almost before he looked up and, when he did, he saw a tall, attractive young lady standing at the counter. She had fine features, short dark hair just visible underneath a blue cloche hat. She was wearing a fashionable silk summer dress in peach and white, and Sergeant Pell thought idly that it looked extremely expensive.

He straightened his tunic subconsciously, putting a hand up to flatten his moustache. He had a habit, when he was bored, of chewing the ends which made them moist and stick out at unprofessional angles.

'Good afternoon Miss. Can I help you?'

Kitty allowed herself an inward smile. It was clear Sergeant Pell didn't in anyway associate the sophisticated woman in front of him with the dowdy, plain-faced Edie Dearlove.

'Good afternoon, Sergeant,' she said. 'I wonder if I may speak with Constable Keyse?'

'I'm sorry Miss, he's out.'

He glanced at the large black clock on the far wall.

'I'm not expecting him back for at least another hour. Is there something I can help with?'

Kitty reached over and covered Sergeant Pell's meaty hand with her delicate fingers. His face flushed a bright shade of pink.

'How sweet of you to ask, but no thank you. It's Constable Keyse I need to speak with. He's looking into a rather sensitive matter for me. Do you know where he might be?'

'Um, I'm not sure I'd know Miss, but you could try over towards the war memorial or perhaps the pavilion. If not, try the fair. Always a good place to winkle out the criminal lower orders, if you know what I mean?'

'Absolutely. Thank you, Sergeant.' Kitty stared directly at the officer but there wasn't the slightest hint of recognition. 'You've been most helpful.'

Outside, Nora and Kitty set off in the direction of the war memorial. There was no sign of Jimmy there but, as they passed the pavilion, they saw his familiar figure standing by the entrance to the fair which decamped onto their little green each July, a chaotic mixture of fairground stalls, booths and kiosks, jostling together noisily and to the delight of a great many holidaymakers.

'Jimmy!' Nora shouted, waving, and he turned around, raising a hand in acknowledgement.

'Hello you two,' he said as they reached him. 'Have you been following me?'

'Of course not, but I did go into the station and Sergeant Pell said we might find you here.'

'Oh,' said Jimmy with a grimace. 'That was brave. Did he recognise you?'

Kitty linked her arm through Jimmy's and leant into him playfully. 'Of course not, silly. I told you I was a good actress and a mistress of disguise.'

Jimmy untangled Kitty's arm from his.

'Not while I'm on duty, Kitty,' he said, looking around to see if anyone had noticed.

'I've been on tenterhooks since Tuesday. I even rang the house this morning. Auntie Elsie said you'd gone out in Betty yesterday, dress shopping. I didn't believe that for a minute, not when we're in the middle of something like this.'

'Haha,' replied Nora, 'we'll make a detective of you yet Constable Keyse!'

'So, don't keep me in suspense. Where've you been? Was it something that William said on Tuesday about his sister?'

'Absolutely. We went over to talk to her.'

'I presume you came clean?' asked Jimmy.

Kitty nodded.

'I imagine she was a little bamboozled by the sight of the two of you. Double trouble and no mistake.'

'She was to start with but we explained who we are and why we were there, and she soon lost that rather befuddled look that most people get when they meet us together for the first time.'

'Did you find out who this mysterious man friend of hers is?'

Nora's sigh felt more frustrated than annoyed. 'She did admit it, which is one thing, but point blank refused to say who he is. She's adamant he wouldn't have had anything to do with any of this horrible business. Apparently, he's a respectable man and she swore that he wouldn't be involved.'

'Yes, and despite Nora's best efforts at coercion and blackmail, she wasn't to be budged,' added Kitty. 'We promised her we wouldn't say anything, so you can't either Jimmy.'

Jimmy considered it for a moment. 'Hard not to now I know, but I trust your judgement. Did she say anything else of any note?'

'Interestingly, she said William thought he might have met that Edward character in jail when they were younger but wasn't sure. I hope you were taking mental notes in the cell when you were studiously looking like you weren't even paying attention, Jimmy?'

'Of course. I did a bit of digging on Edward Keane. He's a fisherman now, seems legitimate, but he has quite a shady past. Nothing violent but has been known to be a bit light-fingered. I can't see him murdering Miss Watcombe but not a bad fit for the pearls.'

'What about a Mr Frank Fogwill? Apparently, he's the landlord at The Ketch Inn. Do you know him?'

'Why?'

'I'll tell you in a minute.'

'Yes, I do know him. His wife Edna used to be quite good

friends with my Mum when they lived over in Paignton, long before they bought the inn.

'I heard he was quite a lad back in the day. Never afraid of a bit of wartime wheeling and dealing. I also found out he'd been invalided out before he'd even got to the boats. He was always the person to go to for extra bits and bobs you couldn't get elsewhere. I think he even served some time for handling stolen goods but it was a long time ago.'

'Do you know who was first on the scene of the murder?' asked Kitty.

'It was Frank, Ed, William and Sergeant Temple of course. But I think we can discount the Sergeant, don't you?'

'Of course, but why didn't the police take a closer look at Ed and Frank when they realised the pearls were missing? Surely they should have been high on the list of suspects given their past lives?'

Jimmy pondered what seemed like a completely reasonable challenge.

'Frank's turned his life around by all accounts. He's been living the life of a respectable publican for years.'

'I still don't get it,' said Kitty. 'There were three of them in the room when the murder was discovered, so any of them could have taken the pearls.'

'Four of them if you include Sergeant Temple,' added Nora.

'But there's the rub, Kitty,' said Jimmy slowly. 'We know Miss Warcombe only took her pearls off at night. I can't believe even Ed or Frank would have been so brazen as to steal them off a dead body, right under the nose of a policeman.'

'That's true, I agree,' said Kitty. 'There could only be one possible explanation.'

Jimmy nodded. 'If we think Ed or Frank took the pearls, they would have had to do it at the same time as they committed the murder.'

The three friends stood in silence for a moment.

'I think I know why they didn't look at Frank and Edward as possible suspects,' said Nora.

'Why?'

'Well, William's an outsider, isn't he? Everyone knows Frank and Edward. They may have had less than auspicious starts in life, but they are part of this community. Well respected now, after a fashion. Surely it's inconceivable to the police that two such upstanding civilians could have done something so wicked?'

'Anyway Kitty, why did you want to know about Frank?' asked Jimmy.

'Jean said something about him having a falling out with Miss Watcombe. Not clear what exactly, but seems he was trying to persuade her to sell her house and land to him. Could have been a motive to kill her.'

'Perhaps the temptation was too great for him,' added Nora. 'He knew he was never going to get the land for his new holiday chalets and car park while she was alive. How convenient if she ends up dead. With no relatives to speak of, the house and land would soon be put up for sale and Frank could be first in the queue.'

'And if he wanted to demolish the house anyway, wouldn't the easiest thing be to set fire to it and hope it burned to the ground? If he's been in prison he's going to be quite wise about these things. Destroy the evidence and bring down the price of the property at the same time,' added Jimmy.

'Exactly,' said Kitty and Nora together.

'If Frank did do it, thank goodness he wasn't as good an arsonist as he was a thief then,' concluded Jimmy.

'What time are you off shift today?' asked Kitty.

Jimmy's eyes narrowed. 'Four. Why?'

'I think it would be useful for someone who knows him to have a friendly word with Frank. Nothing official, just someone who pops in for a drink and gets chatting about the awful events at Rockcliffe House.'

'So you want me to go to The Ketch and casually do a bit of digging around?'

'What a good idea, Jimmy, I wish I'd thought of that!' Kitty said, and the three laughed.

'Perhaps make it seem like you think William's guilty, like everyone else. See if it gets Frank on side, makes him let his guard down.'

'I don't suppose it'd do any harm,' Jimmy pondered. 'I could say I was passing and fancied a pint. Keep it light and see if he says anything incriminating.'

'Excellent. If it's not Frank, perhaps he'll give you some information into Ed's whereabouts and demeanour that night instead,' agreed Nora.

'When can we get together so I can tell you what I find out?'

'Well, we're both working tomorrow, and then we're off to Sir Charles's for dinner. But we could do first thing if you're free?'

'Perfect. I'm on an early shift tomorrow. I'll pop in before work if that's all right? I'll think of a reason why I've got to see Auntie Elsie. I'll come around the back so make sure you're in the kitchen about nine o'clock.'

Kitty and Nora both knew it was Jimmy who was most at

risk from anyone finding out what they were doing. If they got caught, people would just be indulgent towards them. They would hear the same thing they'd been hearing since they were eighteen. About time those two pretty girls found themselves suitable husbands and had babies and stopped all this silly detective nonsense.

But, if Jimmy were caught, they knew he would be treated much more harshly.

Kitty could hear the clamour of voices now.

We can't have him making us look stupid; How dare he make unfounded allegations against upstanding members of this community; Honestly, investigating on his own, who does he think he is?; He'll never be one of us; He's not fit to wear the uniform.

'I love you James Keyse,' said Kitty and Jimmy smiled, not a little embarrassed.

'I mean like a brother, obviously,' she clarified. 'I don't suppose a hug would be acceptable right now, would it? Not with you in uniform and all that.'

Jimmy smiled even more broadly.

'Absolutely not, Miss.'

15

Ham and tomato and extra mustard

Jimmy arrived home just after five thirty.

As he did every day after work, he had walked from the police station in Cedar Road and down into town to catch the number 22 bus from Torquay to Paignton, alighting at the sea front at the start of Esplanade Drive.

He walked up and away from the water and, three roads further back, turned into Barcombe Avenue where he lived with his mother Iris and his grandmother Violet.

Mrs Jones across the street was washing her step and waved hello when she saw him. Such a lovely young man, and what a reassurance to have a policeman in the Avenue.

Jimmy waved back with a smile.

Their house was small and tidy, not pretty but not completely utilitarian either. Despite the grey pebbledash which was peeling in places, his mother insisted on a few colourful annuals along the fence by the pavement, just some petunias or zinnias, whatever she could find, to cheer the place up.

Jimmy put his key in the door and winced at the rush of hot air that greeted him as it did every day, summer or winter.

His granny Vi had a particularly strong aversion to cold and draughts, so the windows were always kept tightly shut. In summer, the heat permeated the little house and had no means of escape. In winter, with the fire ablaze, Jimmy had often had to stand at the bottom of their little garden, on one pretence or another, just to avoid certain death from overheating.

His mother still could not understand why, on Christmas Day 1928, a red-faced and sweating Jimmy had insisted on going outside to creosote the garden shed.

Jimmy did not mind though. His mother and granny were good-hearted souls who spoilt Jimmy despite his frequent assurances that he was a grown man and could do his own darning, cooking and laundry now. It was only last year that he'd managed to convince his mother that he could make his own bed.

'Hi Mum, it's me,' he shouted as he did whenever he came home. Since he had joined the police force, and despite their protestations that they were perfectly safe, he now insisted they kept their front door locked and didn't let in any strangers.

For Iris and Vi, this seemed a silly idea, as if locking your door somehow implied you lived in an unsafe neighbourhood.

'I lived through the war and never once locked my door,' his granny had asserted, 'even though we could all have been murdered in our beds by Fritz.'

Jimmy didn't have the heart to tell her that was extremely unlikely, but he wasn't to be swayed and, after a few weeks when they occasionally forgot, they now turned the latch like clockwork, to please Jimmy if nothing else.

'Hello son,' his mother said, coming out of the back kitchen, wiping her floury hands down the front of her apron. 'I was just making a crumble. We got given some blackberries by Johnny Thompson, he'd picked far more than his mum needed.'

She helped him off with his uniform, hanging his tunic on a hook and setting his helmet down on the little hall table, ready for the morning.

'Cuppa?'

'Oh, yes please,' Jimmy said, following his mother into the kitchen.

Vi was sitting in her chair by the cold hearth, her feet on an embroidered stool, her hands moving remarkably fast over her knitting.

'Hello granny,' he said, stooping down to kiss the top of her head. She smelled of coal tar soap and pear drops. 'How's the scarf coming on?'

'It's a jumper, cheeky!' she replied, holding it up so he could see. *Looks like a scarf to me*, Jimmy thought. 'So it is, lovely too. Who's it for?'

He held his breath. *Don't say for me.*

'I'm making it for Mr Clements down the road. Since his wife departed, poor soul, he hasn't got anyone to look after him and I can't abide the thought of him freezing to death in that cold house in the winter.'

Being as the English Riviera was renowned for its mild winters, Jimmy thought the chance of Mr Clements freezing to death wasn't great but he was sure their elderly neighbour would appreciate such a kind gesture anyway, even if he secretly kept it for his poodle to sleep on.

Iris was busying herself at the stove. 'It's ham and boiled potatoes for tea if that's all right. I could do some cabbage if you'd like?'

Jimmy glanced at the wall clock.

'Actually, mum, if it's okay, I think I'll skip tea tonight.'

Iris's brow furrowed and she rushed over to put her palm on his forehead. He felt reassuringly cool but Jimmy turning down food was a sure sign of impending illness.

'Are you feeling poorly, love?'

He laughed. 'No, never felt better. I just said I'd meet a few colleagues from work in town for a quick drink. Celebrate one of them getting his promotion to sergeant.'

Iris's brow furrowed more deeply, and even Violet looked up from her wool.

'On a work night?'

'It'll only be a swift half. I've got to keep in with the team, Mum, you know that. Don't want them thinking I'm a party-pooper.'

'If you're sure. I can do you a ham sandwich before you go if you like? You shouldn't be drinking on an empty stomach.'

'Thanks, that'll be lovely. I'm just going up to change and wash up. I'll be down in ten minutes.'

Never more happy than when she was feeding her boy, Iris put the chopping board and bread knife on the kitchen table, and went through to the larder to get the loaf.

16

Last orders, gentlemen, please

Jimmy pulled the front door to and turned away from the sea, feeling suitably replete after two large mugs of tea and a ham and tomato sandwich with extra mustard.

He could have retraced his steps from work, catching the number 22 back into the town centre and walking the rest of the way, but he knew if he caught the number 49 from outside the Playhouse it would save him a few minutes and drop him right at the top of Smugglers' Cove Road.

The bus appeared less than a minute after he had reached the stop and he was soon deposited on the main road that led into Wellesmead. To both sides were rows of houses, most terraced but a few semi-detached and the odd bed and breakfast establishment. On the right, partly concealed, was a small opening that was the start of the long, steep road down towards The Ketch Inn.

As he walked, trying to ignore a strange compulsion to topple forward on the steep gradient, he wasn't surprised that the other end of the cove had become so much more popular with visitors after the introduction of the funicular. While the walk down to the inn felt somewhat vertiginous, he knew it was the long drag back up the hill that put off most people from venturing down this way in the first place.

It had been a hot summer day but was now cooling, and a gentle sea breeze ruffled his hair as he walked. He had to admit the view from up here was spectacular. He could see the horizon stretching endlessly from the high cliffs behind the peninsula all the way towards the beaches of Dorset.

As he rounded the last bend, he could see the roof of the Inn almost at his feet as it nestled precariously on the tiny quayside at the bottom of the slope.

A car driver beeped their horn and passed him slowly, coming to rest half on and half off the verge at the bottom. That's definitely the future, Jimmy thought, so perhaps Jean's recollection that Frank and Miss Watcombe had fallen out over a piece of land wasn't quite as far-fetched as it might initially have seemed.

The little stone pier that led into the sea almost perpendicularly from the gate into the inn was quiet, just a couple of hardy anglers already setting up to try their luck at night-time fishing for bass or ray.

The door of the inn was propped ajar with a large stoneware beer flagon to let out some heat and let in some breeze.

Unfortunately, the open door didn't let much light in and, as Jimmy entered, it took his eyes a moment to get accustomed to the gloom.

There were two men in one corner, dressed in rough serge jackets and thick trousers despite the warmth, the sound of their shuffling dominoes filling the space. A rather unprepossessing lurcher cross sat patiently by the side of one of the men and two half emptied glasses of beer sat in soggy puddles on either side of the scarred wooden table. The shuffling stopped and the men chose their tiles without looking up.

A younger man with rheumy eyes and a wispy beard was sitting in one corner with a plain girl with red hair, two small glasses of dark liquid in front of them. They glanced up as Jimmy entered but soon turned their attention away, their heads low together as if they were discussing something that obviously wasn't intended for anyone else's ears.

Another man, older but similarly dressed in fisherman's garb, was sitting at the bar draining his glass as Jimmy approached. He stood up, grunting a farewell to Frank Fogwill who was standing behind the bar polishing glasses, and passed Jimmy towards the door.

Frank looked up.

'Well, look what the tide's washed up! If it isn't little James Keyse. Haven't seen you around here in a while, Jimmy. To what do we owe this pleasure?'

'Hello, Frank,' said Jimmy, resting his palms on the bar. 'I was just passing.'

Frank threw back his head and laughed. 'Nobody just *passes* the Ketch Jimmy, not at this time of an evening. Takes a determined sort of drinker to fancy the walk down and back up again in the dark when they can go to The Old Oak up on the main road.'

Frank looked around the room, seeming wistful.

'Can't remember the last time a stranger came in here at night. Honestly, I think I should just leave this lot their drinks lined up on the bar and go and put my feet up.'

He held up the recently drained glass.

'Pint for Charlie. Pint for Maurice and a pint and a whisky chaser for Peter over there and some pork scratchings for his dog, port and lemon for Ed and Nelly in the corner.' Frank glanced at his watch, mixing a drink in a half pint glass.

'And Reg will be in at quarter past for his shandy, half only on account of his blood pressure.' He put the drink down on the bar in anticipation.

'So, young Jimmy, you are a welcome sight regardless of what brought you here. What'll it be?'

'I'll take a half of best please Frank.'

Frank laughed again. 'Well, that's my retirement fund sorted,' he said. 'Coming up. Do you want to get a table or are you happy at the bar?'

'Oh, I'm happy here thanks Frank if that's okay?'

Frank poured Jimmy's drink and put it in front of him.

'You're not here on official business, are you? Sort of an undercover mission?'

Jimmy smiled and took a long gulp of beer. 'No, not tonight Frank.'

Frank relaxed a bit. 'Didn't think you would be, but you know the boys around here. Haven't been any smugglers for at least a hundred years but some of them still get a bit twitchy in the presence of the law.'

Jimmy held up two fingers. 'Scout's honour, I'm strictly off duty.'

He took two more large mouthfuls of beer and realised he had almost drunk the entire glass.

'Fancy another one?'

Jimmy wanted to keep a clear head but the cold beer was going down a treat.

'Go on then, but just another half and then that's my limit. I'm working in the morning and mum will kill me if I go home tipsy.'

'How is Iris? Keeping well?'

'Very well thanks.'

'And Vi?'

'Yes, both as fit as fleas.'

'Ah, pleased to hear it. Your mum and granny were always so good to me and Edna when we lived over that way. Make sure you pass on our best wishes when you get home.'

'I'll do that.'

Frank busied himself at the bar for five minutes, rearranging the glasses, while Jimmy sat in watchful silence.

Knowing Frank, Jimmy felt he was bound to ask about the investigation and he certainly didn't want to arouse suspicion by mentioning it first. What was the saying, *slowly slowly catchy monkey*?

Reg turned up exactly as predicted on the quarter hour, picked up the shandy which was warming on the bar ready, dropped a few pennies on the counter and went to sit on the opposite side from the domino players, all without a word to Frank.

Frank lent towards Jimmy. 'See what I mean?' he joked, picking up the coins from a puddle of bitter and dropping them in the till without wiping them.

'So, how's the investigation going, you know, that terrible business over at Rockcliffe last week?'

Jimmy suppressed a smile.

'Not much investigating to do. Seems like an open and shut case by all accounts. Neck's our only suspect and plenty of evidence pointing right at him, no mistake. I heard he's off to Exeter next week ready for his trial, although why the county is wasting money on something like that when the outcome's so obvious, beats me.'

'Dare say we won't see him around here again,' said Frank.

Jimmy shook his head. 'No, I imagine his next port of call after the courthouse will be with the hangman'. He remembered William's own words. 'And good riddance to bad rubbish I say!'

Frank poured himself a half of cider, and they clinked glasses. Brothers-in-arms.

Jimmy took another sip of beer, slower this time. Make it last.

'I saw you over at the inquest on Saturday. Rum business but I suppose it has to be done. I heard you might be up for some sort of Chief Constable's commendation, you know, for your quick thinking in getting the water pump up and working before the fire engine arrived.'

Frank waved his hand. 'It was nothing,' he said, hoping it wasn't true about the commendation. Edna would want a new hat.

'And as for going into the house first. Must have been a horrible sight?'

Frank started cleaning more glasses. 'Horrible,' he agreed, a look of slight revulsion on his face. 'I saw enough of that carnage in the war to last me a lifetime.'

Funny, thought Jimmy, *I'd heard he didn't even make it to the front line. Something about spraining his ankle on a kerb stone as he was set to march down to the boat.* He parked that thought. Had Frank Fogwill deliberately created an altered reality of his time during the war and was that the only part of his life that was a fantasy?

'Yes, it must have been terrible. The war and the murder scene I mean. I wish I could have seen it, the murder scene that is, not the war.'

'Trust me lad, you're better off not seeing something like that. That poor old woman, dead as a doornail. And the smell was awful. Fuel and smoke and God knows what else. I don't think I'll ever forget it.'

'You've lived here a long time Frank,' said Jimmy, pondering the subject. 'Presume there wasn't anyone else you think could have been involved? We're still fretting on those lost pearls and can't for the life of us figure out where William would have put them. We wonder if he might have had an accomplice.'

'I shouldn't worry about them. Probably tucked behind a loose skirting board or shoved into the lining of the curtains. Wouldn't be surprised if Nelly over there didn't put her hand in the flour jar when they're all allowed back in and finds them there.'

'I suppose you're right,' agreed Jimmy. 'Would be nice to know though. We don't need them but it would certainly put the last nail in Neck's coffin.'

Jimmy looked over to the couple in the corner.

'Did you say that was Nelly, Nelly Crouch? I thought I recognised her from the inquest.'

'The very same.'

'She looked terrified giving her evidence, didn't she?' said Jimmy.

'Hardly surprising. She was terrible though, wasn't she? I was too although I think I managed to hide it better than she did. That Coroner - what was his name - Moxley, Monkhay?'

'Moxhay.'

'Ah, Moxhay, that's right. He's a scary character and no mistake.'

'I hope she's better prepared for what's to come at the trial, otherwise she'll be a jabbering wreck by the time the defence have finished with her.'

As they spoke, Nelly Crouch got up, the eyes of the man she was with following her all the way to the bar.

Nelly eyed Jimmy suspiciously before turning her gaze back to Frank.

'Two more please Frank,' she said. Frank turned and walked to the furthest end of the bar to retrieve the port.

Jimmy put on his biggest, friendliest smile. 'You're Nelly Crouch aren't you?'

'Aye, and you're Constable Keyse from the top end, aren't you?' she replied, her hard, plain features set firm, her eyes blank.

Jimmy had heard that expression before from those who lived in the relative isolation of Smugglers' Cove, referring to the rest of Wellesmead that lived high up away from the beach.

'Correct, but not tonight. I'm off duty, just enjoying a beer.'

Jimmy took another sip.

'I saw you at the inquest. I must say, I thought you did a splendid job, especially given how formidable Coroner Moxhay can be.'

Nelly's face relaxed slightly, unable to stop herself feeling ever so slightly flattered.

'Thank you. I thought I was terrible but it's nice to hear.'

'No, I'm being honest. You were very calm, especially considering what a terrible ordeal you've been through. You gave a very good account of yourself and what had happened. Well done.'

A small sliver of a smile played on Nelly's lips.

'Here,' said Jimmy taking out his wallet as Frank returned with the drinks. 'I'll pay for those. Money must be a bit tight now you can't work.'

The small smile now became a lot broader, and Jimmy tried not to focus too much on her blackened front teeth.

'Thanks. Yes, it's not easy but Ed and I are managing with what he brings in and I'm looking for new work anyway.'

At the mention of his name, the young man with the rheumy eyes and wispy beard got up and joined them at the bar. Nelly's somewhat alarmingly flirtatious smile instantly died on her lips.

The man picked up both drinks, staring menacingly at Jimmy. 'Come away Nelly. I don't want you talking to strangers.'

Jimmy stared back, his features fixed. *I know who you are Edward Keane, and I know you know I'm the police*, he thought to himself.

The couple sat back down at the far side of the room and exchanged some words. Jimmy couldn't hear what they were saying but the man was obviously angry and Jimmy could see Nelly cowering back in her chair.

They drained their drinks quickly and stood up together. The man took Nelly's upper arm and Jimmy heard her say, 'Ow, Ed, stop it, you're hurting me!' and he released his grip and put his hand on her shoulder.

'Thanks Frank,' he said as they passed the bar, the man shepherding Nelly in front of him, his dark, cold eyes never leaving Jimmy's face. 'See you tomorrow.'

Frank waved absentmindedly as they left.

'Was it something I said?' asked Jimmy lightly, although he couldn't help feeling he'd been looking into the eyes of someone who had the capacity to be controlling, even cruel.

'Don't mind Ed,' laughed Frank. 'Likes to think of himself as a bit of a hard man but I imagine he'd run a mile in a proper fight. All talk, no trousers, that one.'

'Is that the same Edward Keane that Sergeant Temple mentioned at the inquest? The one that went into the house with you and Neck?'

'The very same. Don't think he wanted to, he was just standing in the wrong place at the wrong time, and he wasn't going to say no to the police, not with his record.'

'Record? Oh, he's been in trouble before?'

'A long time ago I think. Bit of this, bit of that, you know, just to make ends meet. Did some time back in the day when he was younger and more stupid. I think he's turned his life around since he got into fishing but, like I said, some of the lads around here still aren't best friends with the law, if you know what I mean. Even those ones who haven't been on the wrong side of it like young Ed don't want to talk to you folk.'

'Well, it was good that Nelly saw Neck stealing the plate otherwise we might have been taking a closer look at the charming Edward Keane,' said Jimmy.

Frank shrugged. 'I'm sure she did, but I might have taken that with a pinch of salt if I were you boys. Wouldn't have put it past Ed just to get a bit of an insurance policy. You know, get Nelly to tell you lot that she saw Neck take the plate and hide it so you didn't cast your eyes in his direction. And probably didn't matter anyway. He'd already been arrested and they'd found the plate so, as you said, another nail in the coffin just means there isn't any chance of that little bastard going unpunished. Mind my French. Nothing wrong with a little bit of embellishment to help him on his way to the trap door, if you get my drift?'

'Perfectly. Anyway Frank,' Jimmy said, lightheartedly, 'my mum said you were a bit of a Jack the Lad yourself back in the day.'

'She's not wrong. I admit I did a few things I'm not proud of but lots of us did then. It was hard to find work after the war, and you've got to make ends meet. I did my time so I don't think I owe society anything. And when Edna came into that bit of money and we bought this place, I've never looked back.'

'Is trade good?'

Frank looked around the inn affectionately. 'I'll be honest, Jimmy, it's not brilliant but not bad either, particularly in the summer. Now the funicular's on the other side of the bay, we do get the odd intrepid tourist coming along the coast path for a pint at lunchtime before heading back. Not so good in the winter though, and not many are brave enough to walk down the hill like you did.'

'I saw a car pass me when I was coming down,' said Jimmy. 'Seems like that's the future, don't you think?'

Frank's eyes lit up. 'I couldn't agree more! I'm always telling Edna, if people could drive down to the inn and back up again, we'd do a roaring trade, what with the lovely view and everything.'

Jimmy looked out of the window. 'Yes, it's beautiful all right, but a bit tight for space. Perhaps when Rockcliffe House comes on the market, you can put a bid in for the garden. Make a good place to park. Never could see the point of Miss Watcombe having such a lot of space. Just more work I reckon.'

'What have you heard?'

Jimmy looked genuinely puzzled. He sometimes hated his boyish good looks, but his air of innocence and guilelessness had stood him in good stead in many a tight spot.

He shook his head. 'Nothing, why?'

Frank relaxed. 'Never mind. But, yes, you're right, might be a possibility. I hadn't thought of it before but I'll bear it in mind.'

Frank changed the subject.

'When did you say you think Neck will be going to Exeter?'

'Not sure, but I've heard it'll probably be next week,' Jimmy replied.

'Have you spoken with him since he's been locked up with you lot?'

'Yes, a couple of times. Mostly *here's your dinner, Neck, here's a clean blanket, Neck,* That sort of thing. Seemed pleasant enough but then, I've never met a proper murderer before. I thought he might have two heads, or horns or a pointy tail, but he doesn't. He just seems like a normal lad.

'You knew him, didn't you? What did you think of him?' Jimmy added.

'He was nice enough, I suppose. Seemed hard working. I heard from Jean he'd had a bit of bad luck in the past but then who hasn't?'

'And what about Jean?'

'Ah, the lovely Jean Carmody.' Frank looked wistful, leaning in towards Jimmy and lowering his voice. 'Well, I wouldn't say no, if you know what I mean.' He winked. Boys together.

There was a noise behind Frank.

'Wouldn't say no to what Frank?' a voice said and they both straightened up to see Edna Fogwill emerging from a small door behind the bar that led to their tiny sitting room.

'Nothing my love,' said Frank, turning away and trying to make himself look busy. 'Anyway, look who's here,' he added, thankful to have something to distract her.

Edna looked across the bar at Jimmy. She squealed with delight and clapped her hands together.

'Oh Jimmy Keyse, how lovely to see you!' she exclaimed, coming around to his side and grabbing him in a tight bear hug. Her weighty frame squashed against him and he could feel her ample, matronly breasts pressing into his stomach.

Edna Fogwill was what his granny Vi would have called a proper 'Devonshire Dumpling.' Short and exceedingly round, her moon-face and neck disappearing under folds of double chins and her arms heavy with fat. Jimmy knew she had once been an attractive – and much slimmer – woman, and he could still see some of that past glory beneath the thread veins on her red cheeks, especially when she smiled broadly, as she was now doing.

She pulled away slightly.

'My, haven't you grown? And so handsome. Sometimes I see you across the street when I'm up town and I say to Frank, gosh, doesn't Iris's son look dashing in that uniform of his. Anyway, Jimmy, what brings you here?'

Frank coughed. 'He said he was just passing.'

'Just passing?' Edna's crepey eyes crinkled. 'Don't be daft. No one ever just passes The Ketch in the evening.'

Jimmy laughed.

'Funnily enough, I heard those exact words from Frank

when I got here Edna. Honestly, I was just walking back into town from visiting Auntie Elsie up at the Markham's place and I fancied a pint. Rather give you my trade than those out-of-towners up top, and I enjoy the walk anyway.'

'Really?' Edna said, still sceptical. 'Well, whatever the reason, it's lovely to see you. I hope Frank's been looking after you?'

Jimmy drained his glass. 'Expertly, thanks.' He reached into his pocket and put some coins on the bar. 'Oh, put your money away Jimmy,' said Edna. 'On us.'

'No, I insist Edna, thanks all the same,' said Jimmy, picking up the coins and depositing them into Frank's outstretched hand.

'Police Constables mustn't be seen to be accepting favours from friends or anyone else for that matter. We need to maintain our impartiality at all costs even if that means turning down a free pint here and there.'

'Very glad to hear it,' said Frank. 'If the police become as corruptible as the rest of us, where would we be?'

Edna slapped his arm playfully, but her glare said *don't give him ideas, we're respectable folk now.*

Jimmy looked at his watch.

'I'd better be off. Don't want to miss the last bus and Mum will only wait up worrying if I'm not back on time.'

As he turned to leave, Jimmy noticed a dark cane in the hatstand by the open door. The broken top of the cane caught his eye. There was a tapered end of unstained wood where a finial cap had once been.

'Here, Frank,' he said back over his shoulder. 'Not sure who's cane that is, but I think they've lost the top. Hope it wasn't expensive.'

Frank glanced over. 'Oh, don't worry, that's mine. Cost me a pretty penny from Clarkenhall's last year. Only used it twice and the bloody top came off. I've never found it, more's the pity.'

'Silver, was it?' asked Jimmy. 'Do you want me to take a description so I can make a note back at the station in case anyone hands it in?'

'Don't worry Jimmy. It'll be long gone. I'll use the money you gave me for those two half pints to buy a new gold one, perhaps with a diamond in it!' Frank chuckled at his own joke.

'I don't think you will,' Edna said forcefully, not sure whether her husband was being serious or not. Her smile didn't quite reach her eyes as she looked at Frank and then turned back towards Jimmy.

'A silver topped cane, what nonsense! I'm sure we could have spent that money on something more useful, perhaps a new bed or one of those new-fangled vacuum cleaners, but you know Frank.' *Well, I thought I did, just a bit,* pondered Jimmy, *but now I'm not so sure.*

'Always fancied himself as Lord of the Manor,' she muttered quietly, almost to herself.

'Anyway,' she added, the thought instantly forgotten. 'Don't make it so long before we see you again Jimmy. And don't forget to say hello to Iris and Vi from us both. The next time I'm over in Paignton, tell Iris I'll pop in for a cuppa.'

'I won't and thanks, she'd like that. Bye Frank, bye Edna.'

With that, Jimmy walked out into the gathering summer dusk and girded himself for the steep climb back up to the bus stop.

17

Pass the tea towel

Mrs Lockhart stared at the kitchen clock then at Kitty and Nora and then back at the clock. It read six minutes past nine which she knew was accurate as the kitchen clock kept excellent time.

As usual, Kitty and Nora had brought the breakfast plates and crockery through from the dining room but, instead of just putting them in the sink as they always did for Mrs Lockhart to do later, Kitty had suddenly announced she was happy to do the washing up, quickly followed by Nora who eagerly offered to dry and put away.

As Mrs Lockhart had known them since they were small, she didn't welcome this departure from the status quo. If truth be told, she found it quite alarming.

She had initially tried to bat them away with a *that's thoughtful but no need* and was surprised when they seemed so determined not to be deterred. Before Mrs Lockhart could protest any further, Kitty had already added hot water to the sink from the tea kettle and a handful of lye and began working up some suds.

Kitty glanced at the clock herself. *Come on Jimmy, where are you?* she thought, nibbling her lip nervously.

As Nora grabbed a tea towel and stood guard over the draining board, they heard the back door handle turn and Jimmy appeared. He was dressed in his uniform but his face looked rather pink, as if he had run the last few yards.

Kitty raised her eyebrows in his direction as if to say *about time*!

Mrs Lockhart saw her favourite grandnephew and temporarily forgot her confusion and amazement at seeing Kitty and Nora doing household chores.

'Oh, hello Jimmy. This is a pleasant surprise.'

'Hello Auntie Elsie,' said Jimmy, kissing her on the cheek. 'Hello you two,' he added almost as an afterthought.

'Hello Jimmy. What brings you here at this time of the morning?' said Nora.

'Mum asked me if I could pop in on my way to work. Auntie Elsie, granny says do you have some number 10 knitting needles she can borrow please, and also have you got any purple wool? She's edging a cardy.'

'Hmm…,' Mrs Lockhart thought. 'I've definitely got the needles but I'm not sure about the wool. Give me five minutes and I'll go and have a quick look.'

Without waiting for a response from Jimmy, she left the kitchen.

As soon as the door was closed, Kitty quickly wiped her hands on the tea towel Nora was holding.

'Well?' said Nora.

'I spoke to Frank.'

'Jimmy, make it quick,' said Kitty, getting closer so they could keep their voices low. 'Lockie'll be back in a minute.'

Jimmy took out his policeman's notebook, having written up from memory the conversation he'd had with Frank as soon as he got home yesterday.

He began to read out loud.

'Number 1. Frank said he thought Nelly might be lying about seeing William steal the plate to protect her boyfriend Edward Keane. No evidence to prove that, just his hunch.

'Number 2. Frank freely admitted that both he and Edward had been in trouble with the law before but claims they are both now going straight.

'Number 3. Frank absolutely denied having had any previous thoughts about trying to get his hands on Miss Watcombe's garden to turn it into a car park for the inn.

'Number 4,' he paused, 'this is the really interesting one. Number 4. He has a cane with a missing top. I asked him if it was silver. He didn't confirm that but said it was expensive and he'd just lost it somewhere. I offered to record it at the police station but he said not to bother, which seemed odd.'

He closed his notebook.

'Oh, and Edna said something strange. She said Frank had always had aspirations to be the Lord of the Manor. What's wrong Nora?'

Nora had her head tilted to one side, thinking.

'That's odd. Do you remember, Kitty, that first morning when we showed Lockie the newspaper? She said almost exactly the same about Jean Carmody. Something about her swanning around as if she wanted to be the Lady of the Manor.'

'Coincidence? Just a figure of speech?' said Jimmy.

'Probably, but slightly strange don't you think?'

Kitty suddenly looked perplexed.

'Perhaps we've been duped, even lied to. Perhaps we've been as misdirected as the police were? What if Frank and Jean are in this together? He sends her off for the night, kills Miss Watcombe, probably steals her pearls and hides them and then, when the dust has settled, leaves Edna for Jean.'

'But didn't Jean tell you that Frank and Edna were the perfect couple?'

Jimmy couldn't help giving a small snort. 'Really? Not what I've heard over the years. My mum said Frank was always a one for the ladies, if you get my drift. And I know from something he said yesterday that he was pretty taken with Jean Carmody.'

'Well, even if he doesn't love Edna, he loves that inn and he would never want to leave it,' said Kitty.

A look of dawning horror spread across Nora's face.

'Oh my goodness. If he's already killed one old lady and got away with it, it wouldn't take much to finish off poor unsuspecting Edna too, would it? Push her down the stairs or slip something into her cocoa, say she's had a heart attack.'

'But I just don't understand,' said Kitty. 'Why would Jean want to incriminate William? Everyone says how much she loves him and has helped him over the years.'

Nora shrugged. 'Or perhaps she and Frank are so devious that they got William there exactly so they could have an unsuspecting stooge to pin the blame onto. Perhaps it was part of some elaborate plan from day one?'

'But it was Jean who told me about the argument between Miss Watcombe and Frank. Why would she have done that?'

It was Jimmy's turn to shrug. 'I don't know. Misdirection perhaps, cause a bit of confusion, muddy the waters? Perhaps she loves William a little after all. Perhaps she wanted to sow just enough doubt, without condemning Frank, to save William.'

'Lord,' said Kitty, blowing out her cheeks. 'It's all so confusing. It was so much more straightforward finding Horus.'

They heard footsteps, and Mrs Lockhart came back into the kitchen holding some knitting needles and a ball of wool. If she noticed how the conversation died instantly and how Kitty, Nora and Jimmy were standing stock still in a small, guilty looking huddle, she didn't say.

She shook her head involuntarily, dispelling a fleeting memory of the time they had broken one of her Meissen figurines when they were much younger and she had gone out to pull up some carrots from the kitchen garden and found them trying to bury the pieces next to the brassicas.

'Here's the needles Vi wants Jimmy,' she said, handing them to him. 'And what about this wool?'

Jimmy took the ball of wool and studied it critically. 'I think that's a bit on the red side, Auntie. Have you got anything with a more pinky tone? I think that would go better with the colours granny's already using.'

Mrs Lockhart's eyes spoke volumes. She could not put her finger on it exactly but the whole universe felt like it had shifted slightly sideways. The Markham twins washing up and her Jimmy suddenly having an interest in colour co-ordination.

She took the ball of wool back from Jimmy, exasperated. 'Here, let me have that. I'll go and take another look.'

As soon as she had shut the door behind her again, Nora said 'So what now? Do you think we've got enough to at least get the police to take another look at the case? Introduce some new suspects? Even just cast a bit of doubt?'

Jimmy shook his head. 'I'm not sure, but I doubt it. All pretty circumstantial.'

Kitty looked at Nora.

'I think we should at least tell someone. How about Sir Charles at dinner tonight. He'll know what to do.'

'I'm not sure,' replied Nora, looking somewhat alarmed at the prospect. 'Papa will literally kill us when he realises what we've been up to.'

'I don't think he'll *literally* kill us, Nora,' said Kitty, although she didn't sound quite as sure as Nora would have liked.

'I know, I know. But I just don't think we can keep this to ourselves. Even if we have the slimmest chance of saving an innocent man, it's got to be worth the risk.'

They heard Mrs Lockhart returning.

'We'll let you know what happens Jimmy,' Kitty said, quickly squeezing his arm reassuringly before turning back to the sink and plunging her arms up to the elbows in the soapy water. She handed Nora a teacup which Nora proceeded to dry with a somewhat overzealous degree of studious attention.

Mrs Lockhart came in holding three balls of wool.

'I thought I'd bring these so you could choose,' she said. Jimmy, hardly looking, selected one at random and shoved it into his pocket along with the needles.

'Thanks Auntie, that's super. I'd better be going or I'm going to get into hot water with the Sarge. I'll let myself out. Bye ladies.'

He disappeared through the door without a backward glance.

Mrs Lockhart turned her undivided attention back to the spectacle of Kitty and Nora and the washing up.

18

In memorium

22nd May 1917

Recommendation (Commanding Officer)
Court Martial - Pte Philip James PARKER

While the defendant initially showed some fortitude under enemy fire, the overall character of Pte Parker is not good.

From a fighting point of view, he is now quite useless and this is his second attempt to get away from his unit, firstly at Neuve Chapelle and now at Rue Petillon. I had, on more than one occasion prior to this incident, strongly ordered him to pull himself together.

At the time of the offence with which he is currently charged, there were two witnesses who attest to the fact that Pte Parker was not seen in the firing line where he was instructed to be and had absented himself from the heat of battle, being apprehended sometime later approximately four miles behind friendly lines.

As a deterrent to others, I would respectfully submit it would be a pity if a lenient view of his recidivist conduct prevailed.

Commanding Officer
Lt. Col. Huxley Pangbourne

23rd May 1917

Recommendation (Physician in Charge)
Court Martial - Pte Philip James PARKER

I confirm I was asked to observe Pte Parker for four days prior to his forthcoming Court Martial and make a medical assessment of his condition.

During my observations, I saw a man who was unable to sleep, suffering from severe headache and with uncontrollable tremors in his hands and legs. Under my questioning, he appeared confused and disassociated. He also exhibited severe physical symptoms, collapsing to the floor and hiding under his bunk at any loud noise such as the slamming of a door. I believed all these manifestations to be genuine.

It is my diagnosis that Pte Parker is suffering from a total mental collapse brought on by an extended period of time at the front line. I recommend that he be returned to England immediately where he can be placed in a secure mental facility and afforded the rest and treatment he requires to recover from this terrible illness.

Dr John Markham

19

Dinner at Glencoe

As Kitty and Nora came down the staircase at exactly seven, they could see their father waiting for them in the hallway.

He looked dashing in his dinner suit, if somewhat uncomfortable. His hair was freshly washed and combed down, albeit an errant piece was sticking up on his crown and Kitty reached up absentmindedly to smooth it down.

'This collar is too tight, I feel like I'm being strangled.' As if to demonstrate, he wiggled his finger into the narrow gap between his tie and neck, pulling at it.

'You look very handsome, papa,' said Nora.

'Do I?' said John Markham fidgeting from foot to foot. He much preferred his comfortable old tweed jacket with the worn leather elbow patches.

'And I'm sure Miss Davey will think so too,' joked Kitty with a wink.

Despite her rigor mortis features, Kitty and Nora could see a certain light in Miss Davey's rather attractive green eyes when she looked at their father. It was not a surprise, they said. *You're an extremely handsome man, papa, well at least for someone quite so old.*

John stepped back to look at his daughters. While their wardrobes were a mystery to him, he could not deny they had turned into sophisticated and beautiful young women, almost without him noticing. *Was it only a few years ago when Caroline used to mark their heights each birthday with a pencil on the kitchen door frame?*

'You both look very nice this evening too,' he said proudly. Kitty had chosen a pale blue chiffon dress patterned with seafoam green fronds, Nora favouring dusky rose silk with black panels and a deep white collar.

'Good enough for dinner at Glencoe, don't you think?'

'Absolutely.' He held out the crook of his arms. 'Shall we?'

The evening was fine and still warm, with a light breeze. Within minutes, they had reached the front door of Glencoe and it was wrenched open rather unceremoniously by Arthur.

'Oh, hello Arthur,' said Nora with a frown. 'We weren't expecting to see you here this evening. Are you joining us for dinner?'

'No, I just wanted to say hello.'

'Hello,' said Kitty and Nora in unison.

Arthur smiled. 'Hello.'

As they spoke, Constance Davey arrived from the back of the house where the kitchen was located. She looked slightly harassed but involuntarily smoothed down her apron on seeing Dr Markham.

'Good evening, Dr Markham, Kitty, Nora. I told Arthur he could answer the door and say hello then go straight off to his room. He can take his supper up there this evening.'

With Arthur duly banished away from the adults, the Markhams were shepherded into the sitting room and were soon joined by Sir Charles, his large frame squeezed into a suit that was probably a little too small but carrying it off much better than John would ever achieve.

The evening was extremely enjoyable, the conversation light and sociable. John and Charles talked about cricket for a while, work, the state of the nation, the trials and tribulations of the minority Labour government. Kitty and Nora lauded Stanley Baldwin for giving women the franchise only two years earlier. They said they hoped it was the start of a revolution for women in the workplace too, a view rebutted by Sir Charles who could not help thinking a woman's place was most definitely in the home and men's work should be left to men.

When politics started to stray more into heated debate than was appropriate for a sociable dinner, John redirected the conversation to the unseasonably hot weather they were having that year and the prospects for the home teams at the upcoming Empire Games.

Talk of sport led Sir Charles to one of his favourite topics, horse racing. He was in an exceedingly good mood having just had some extraordinary luck at the races the weekend before and winning what he described as 'not an inconsiderable sum' backing a no-hoper of a nag that outlasted the favourites on the long run down the home straight, giving him odds of 25-1.

Despite Sir Charles's assertions to the contrary, Miss Davey was an excellent cook, bringing them a delicious chilled white almond soup to start.

'Aye, Connie,' said Sir Charles, wiping his mouth

appreciably after spooning in the last of his main course, the mouthwatering aroma of wine, onions and cream still pervading the air. 'That was a cracking chicken stew and those sweet lumps were delicious.'

Miss Davey's eyes narrowed almost imperceptibly as she stared at Sir Charles.

'It was ragoût de lapin aux pruneaux.'

'Rabbit with prunes,' said John, and Miss Davey's lips twitched. Perhaps not a smile but probably the closest they were going to see tonight.

'Well, rabbit or chicken, it was extremely tasty. Amazing what you can concoct in that cauldron of yours.'

After bringing in a strawberry pavlova for dessert, Miss Davey laid out coffee and petit fours then asked to be excused for the evening, saying she would tidy the rest of the plates away in the morning. With a somewhat dismissive wave of his hand, Sir Charles agreed and Miss Davey left quietly, her only acknowledgement being a slight nod of the head in John Markham's direction.

'You shouldn't be so cruel to Miss Davey, Sir Charles,' said Kitty. 'You'd be absolutely lost without her.'

Sir Charles patted his stomach. 'She knows I don't mean it. Thought I might give her a pay rise soon, show my appreciation.'

'I imagine the money would be welcome, Sir Charles,' added Nora with a shake of her head. 'But I suspect she rather you didn't keep making so many witch references. Watch out, or one day she might just put a hex on you.'

'So, girls, what have you been doing this summer to keep yourself occupied? I hope you're working on your backhand Nora?'

'Yes, it's definitely improving.'

'And Kitty, how's that front crawl coming along? Still struggling with the breathing?'

'Not as much as I was but I think I'll stick to breaststroke. So much more civilised, don't you think? Honestly, one can't abide it when one gets one's hair wet.' She gave a short, sideways glance at Nora with an almost imperceptible smile.

Nora decided to take the bull by the horns.

'Oh, and we've been looking into the case against William Neck.'

There was silence as both Sir Charles and John digested this piece of information.

'We don't think he killed Agnes Watcombe.'

Sir Charles started to laugh but pulled himself up short when he saw that Kitty and Nora were deadly serious.

'You don't honestly think William Neck's an innocent man, do you?'

'Yes we do Sir Charles,' replied Kitty. 'Actually, we've been doing a bit of digging.'

Kitty could feel her father's eyes boring into the side of her head so, despite an almost overwhelming urge to look around, she stared straight at Sir Charles.

'Digging?' he said, looking confused. 'Literally?'

'No, of course not. Metaphorically. We've been looking at the evidence, at least what we've read in the paper, and found out a few more things that might cast some doubt on William's guilt.'

Sir Charles sat back in his chair and took a deep drag of his cigar.

'Kitty, Nora. I know you girls like to play detective. I've seen you inveigle poor Arthur into your scheming on more than one occasion and he could certainly do without the distractions from his studies. But I can tell you the evidence against William Neck is incontrovertible and overwhelming.'

Kitty sighed. 'We know it doesn't look good for him. Don't be cross papa,' she added, unable any longer to resist the urge to turn around and look at her father.

John didn't appear angry as much as resigned and perhaps a little embarrassed that his daughters had apparently broadsided an unsuspecting Sir Charles.

'I'm so sorry about Kitty and Nora,' John started to say but Sir Charles waved his protestations away good-naturedly.

'No matter John. Actually, girls, I'd be intrigued to learn more about what you think you've uncovered. I was going to suggest bridge as we have a four, but why don't we play a little parlour game instead? I'll act for the prosecution, and you can act for the defence, and John here can be the judge and jury. He's got a good, sound mind on him and I imagine very little interest in the outcome so he will be admirably unbiased.'

'Let's put our evidence on the table and we'll see if you've uncovered anything that convinces me I'm wrong. John, bring those cigars would you?'

They wandered through to the drawing room, Sir Charles opening the long French windows to let some of the evening coolness into the room.

'Tawny Port?' Sir Charles asked from the sideboard and poured them all a generous measure.

They settled down into the comfy armchairs. Charles and John on one side of a low Chinese lacquered table, Kitty and Nora the other.

'So, let's agree some rules, shall we?' Traditionally the

prosecution would lay out their entire case first. Do you want me to do that or do you want to rebut as we go along?'

'I think we're happy either way Sir Charles,' said Nora. 'Isn't that right Kitty?'

'Absolutely.'

Sir Charles clapped his hands.

'Excellent. I can probably lay out in a few sentences why Neck is as guilty as Lucifer, why the jury will have no hesitation in convicting him and why he'll swing for his crimes.'

Kitty and Nora thought Sir Charles sounded a little too gleeful at the prospect of William's execution but perhaps that was what happened when you were Chief Constable. Despite legal convention, to a policeman, of whatever rank, everyone was guilty until proven innocent.

Sir Charles got to his feet.

'The case for the prosecution. William Neck, known criminal, killed Miss Agnes Watcombe. He took her pearls and hid them, set fire to the body and thus the house, and then puts himself in the centre of the rescue effort to deflect attention away from himself as the culprit. In terms of material evidence, we have the bloody murder weapon found in his overcoat pocket, a distinct smell of kerosene having been detected on his boots and blood on his jacket and trousers. And we now know that's Group O, just like Miss Watcombe.'

'We also have an eyewitness who saw him steal and conceal a silver plate and no one disputes the fact that he had an argument over money with Miss Watcombe the day prior to the murder.'

Sir Charles looked particularly self-satisfied as he sat

back down in the armchair and took a long congratulatory sip of port.

Nora took out a piece of paper from her handbag which had been folded several times. She smoothed it out on her knee and handed it to Kitty. They had agreed to try and lay out what they knew but, at the same time, being careful not to name anyone else involved. Certainly not Jimmy and Arthur and, if at all possible, avoiding mentioning they had spoken directly to William, Jean and Frank.

Kitty was a much better orator than Nora and could always bring her acting skills to bear if she felt herself wavering under Sir Charles's uncompromising stare. She was going to stay seated but she followed Sir Charles's lead and stood up.

'Sir Charles, you could well be right. William Neck is the perfect candidate for the murderer, and we don't dispute anything you've said. There was an eyewitness regarding the stolen plate, he did argue with the victim, the knife was found in his possession, he did have blood and kerosene on his clothing and he certainly has a criminal past.'

She paused, letting the fact that she was apparently agreeing with everything Sir Charles had said sink in. It seemed to have the desired effect. He sat forward on his chair, intrigued at what was to come if the girls seemed to be implying he was right all along.

'But we contend that there are many elements to this case that, if nothing else, cast doubt on the chain of events and the party or parties involved.'

'Firstly, where are the pearls? They can't just have disappeared into thin air but I imagine, despite the best efforts of your men in searching the house and gardens, there has been no trace of them.'

'Secondly, have you checked William for injuries? Perhaps the blood on his clothing was his? He had been using a hatchet to cut back burning timbers after all.

'And I heard there were no fingerprints on the knife.'

'And who told you that?'

Kitty swallowed down an urge to stammer.

'I can't remember. I think I read it somewhere. Anyway, the point is, if there were no fingerprints, that meant the murderer must have worn gloves. Have you found any gloves in William Neck's possession?'

Sir Charles pondered the question for a moment. 'Actually, I don't think so but that's not hard to explain. He just as likely threw them into the sea or tucked them away in the shrubbery. If the former, we'll never find them.'

Nora interjected from her seat. 'And if the blood on William's clothing was common, like O for instance, who's to say that it isn't William's own blood and not Miss Watcombe's? Has anyone checked?'

'And what about other suspects in the area?' continued Kitty. 'We know of at least two who have similar criminal pasts. Edward Keane and Frank Fogwill. Both were at the scene, and both went into the house with William and your Sergeant Temple when they discovered poor Miss Watcombe's body. Has anyone even looked at them?

'And as for Nelly Crouch's testimony. She could just as easily have made the whole thing up so that you didn't cast your eyes in Edward's direction. He is her boyfriend you know, perhaps she's scared of him and just did what he told her to do.'

Kitty felt she was on a roll as she scanned Nora's handprinted notes.

'And why would William have put the murder weapon in his own pocket?'

'Ah, now Kitty, I must interject on that subject,' said Sir Charles with a smile that was a touch patronising for Kitty's liking.

'The criminal classes aren't like you or me, or Nora or John. They don't think rationally or exercise good judgement or consider the consequences of their actions. As sensible, educated people, we would throw our hands in the air and say 'of course no rational person would do anything so stupid' but, trust me, I've met a lot of much more hardened criminals than young Neck and it has never failed to amaze me how irrational, illogical and downright stupid they can be.'

Kitty exchanged a look with Nora that said, *I know we promised, but I'm going to have to say something.*

'And then there's what we learned from Jean Carmody.'

'You've spoken to Jean Carmody?' said John.

'Yes, last week.'

A look of dawning realisation played across John's face.

'Am I to surmise Kitty that your *friend*, Mary Seal was it, is as mythical a creature as a mermaid and you actually went to see Jean Carmody when you borrowed Betty?' he asked.

'We'll make a detective of you yet papa,' she replied, looking sheepish. 'And it was Myra Searle actually. I'm sorry I lied.'

John got up and poured himself another large port. He felt he needed it.

'She told us she has a lover, a man friend at the very least.'

'Did she say who?' asked Sir Charles, frowning.

'No, and she swore she never would. All she'd say was he

was of good character and we know he has a silver-topped cane.'

'Well that narrows it down a bit, perhaps to several hundreds, perhaps a thousand, Torquinian men!' exclaimed Sir Charles.

Kitty sighed. 'Yes we know. But we're pretty sure the police didn't even know this man existed, so perhaps he could have been someone of interest too.'

'And she also told us that Frank Fogwill had had a major disagreement with Miss Watcombe over a land deal and has a broken cane with the top missing,' added Nora.

Sir Charles seemed to be considering this new information, combing the sides of his bushy grey moustache as he was want to do when he was thinking.

'Did you ever meet Miss Watcombe, girls? You John?'

All three shook their heads.

'No, me neither. I've heard she was a nice old lady, perhaps a bit eccentric at times, but nonetheless kind-hearted. What about Jean Carmody?'

'She's one of my patients. You?'

'I'd never met her before the inquest,' replied Sir Charles. 'Afterwards, I thanked her for coming and we talked for about five minutes. I must say, she's one fine looking lass and no mistake so I'm not surprised she had an admirer.'

Sir Charles thought for a moment, drained his glass and then continued.

'But, honestly girls, I can't see her being involved. By all accounts, she doted on Miss Watcombe and the feeling was apparently mutual. I thought she seemed truthful and genuine, and hell would have to freeze over first before I could see her doing anything so monstrous. Granted, she's got a rather blinkered view of her brother's innocence, but loyalty like that is an admirable quality, if totally misplaced.

'Don't you think that poor woman's been through enough already without any more unsubstantiated rumours and accusations? By every account she's decent and hard-working but she's now vilified by society for her associations and relations, whispered about, ignored. I doubt she'll ever be able to work in this town again.'

'We agree,' said Nora. 'We both like her very much and actually don't think she can be involved. We did speculate for a while that maybe her man friend was Frank Fogwill but it doesn't seem likely. I suppose we just wanted to show how many different possible angles the police could have considered, rather than automatically assuming it was William.'

'And what about Miss Watcombe's will? No one's found that either,' added Kitty, although the fight seemed to have left her a little bit.

'I don't think that's such a big deal Kitty. I've heard from my men who've been in the house that it's a mess. Papers all over the place. Those that weren't damaged by the fire were just as likely to have been damaged by the water. Once Neck has gone over to Exeter, I'm going to allow Miss Carmody back into the house and she can have a proper look around. As like as not, she'll find the will or what's left of it in the debris.'

'So, is that your evidence?'

The twins nodded in unison.

'An excellent defence argument, I must say. I'm sorry and, of course, it'll be down to the jury but, despite all your well thought out challenges, it's not enough to convince me that William Neck isn't the murderer.'

Kitty sat back down with a thump and rather more unladylike than she would have wanted to.

Sir Charles smoothed down his moustache in a most self-congratulatory way.

'Don't be downhearted. With my thirty years of policing experience, I agree Neck could possibly have had an accomplice, so you've done some excellent work. I just wish some of my men were as thorough and diligent as you've been. You never know, one day we might follow the Metropolitan Police, and allow women detectives on the force. As long as they were nice looking young ladies like you. I'll not be employing any middle-aged vinegar spinsters.'

He thought for a moment.

'Assuming Neck killed Miss Watcombe, could someone else have taken the pearls? It's possible. Hide them away until they were both sure they'd got away with it and then divvy up the profits.'

Nora looked perplexed. 'But if that's the case, why hasn't he told anyone? Surely he wouldn't want to face the gallows alone when he knows there's someone else as guilty as him?'

'That's not how it works, Nora, I'm afraid. Honour among thieves and all that. Even if by some fluke he escapes the executioner, if he'd gone down implicating Frank Fogwill or Edward Keane, or any other person with a known criminal past, he'd probably last a week in prison before someone would do him over with a homemade blade or just beat him to death with their bare hands. These low sorts have a strange code of conduct. They could rob you blind and murder you in your bed but woe betide any criminal who pointed the finger at another.'

Sir Charles could see how despondent the Markham

twins looked at this news. All their hard work roundly pooh-poohed by the most senior policeman in the county.

'But I was interested in what you said about the disagreement Frank had with Miss Watcombe. Could be some sort of motive I suppose. And interesting about the cane too.

'Seems a bit above himself for a man of his station, but Frank Fogwill always was a bit of fantasist, wasn't he John? Didn't he tell you once he'd been in France?'

John nodded slowly. 'Yes, I was bandaging an ulcer on his leg and he started telling me this elaborate tale about being in the war. All seemed a bit far-fetched, but I didn't say anything at the time. I found out later, I can't remember how, that he'd never even made it out of England. Health issues I think, but whether real or imaginary we'll never know.'

Sir Charles nodded in agreement.

'He wouldn't have been the first to swing the lead, bloody business that war is. What I'd say about Frank is that he's no one's fool. In my experience, it was the clever ones who got away with things, you know, feigning illness or injury just to keep away from the action.

'Or, worse still, the poor souls who deserted. I heard many a clever, wily one got away with it. It was the stupid ones, or the ones who were genuinely ill who got caught and we know that didn't end well for most of them.'

As a field doctor, John Markham had been present at one such execution at dawn and it had lived with him ever since. Despite his protestations that the young soldier in question was ill, his calls for leniency had fallen on deaf ears. He pushed the memory down and back into the strongbox he called 'Horrors of War' that he kept in his head and closed the lid tightly.

Sir Charles let out an indulgent sigh.

'So Edward Keane might not have been clever enough to commit this crime, but it seems Frank Fogwill could have been, or maybe they were both involved, him and Neck.

'I'll tell you what I'll do girls. I can't see someone of such low orders as Edward Keane to have the intelligence to pull off something that audacious, but I'll get someone to take a closer look at Frank. Maybe get a couple of constables to go down to the inn, lean on him a bit, find out what he knows. If he's not hiding anything, we're no worse off than we are today.'

There was a moment of silence.

'Well, Judge Markham, you've heard the evidence before you today. What is the verdict of you and the jury?'

John's cigar had been sitting unsmoked between his fingers and he lent forward and propped it on the side of a large green onyx ashtray.

He had listened intently to both sides, despite his initial annoyance that his daughters had, once again, gone against his express wishes.

He sometimes talked to Caroline in his head and he could well imagine the conversation. *Caroline, they're getting terribly headstrong.*

Caroline would have kissed him and patted his hand. *Absurdité, John, they're just becoming the two independently minded young women we always hoped they would be. It's the future, you know.*

John looked up from his reverie.

'I agree with Kitty and Nora.'

He glanced at his daughters. They smiled at their father.

'It's those blasted pearls, Charles. Where are the pearls?

Without them, there's always going to be some lingering doubt. Trust me Charles, there isn't anything like the guilt you live with when you can't save an innocent man's life.'

'I wouldn't know John, but one thing I am sure about and that's the guilt of William Neck. Never was a criminal I sent to the gallows who didn't deserve it. No room for your liberal sensibilities here, I'm afraid. He did it, as heck as like, and I'll sleep like a newborn baby in my bed the night after he's gone to meet his maker.

'And as for the pearls, I'll grant it, you're right. It is a bit of an annoying loose end that I wish we didn't have. But, mark my words, Jean Carmody will just as likely find them in Miss Watcombe's night stand or down the back of the dressing table, and the only thing I'll have to worry about then is giving my men a right royal rollocking for being so useless and lackadaisical. Either that, or some unsuspecting tourist will find them ten years hence in a gully or under some stones up in the wood behind the Rock where Neck had hidden them all along.'

The debate seemed to have run its natural course, both sides felt like they had won and lost in equal measure. Kitty and Nora were disappointed that Sir Charles did not think they had found enough to overturn William's guilt but were pleased to have their father's support, and Sir Charles was similarly disappointed to have lost the jury vote to the Markham girls but had in no way been shaken from his absolute self-belief in knowing that William Neck was the murderer.

As they said their goodnights at the front door, Sir Charles seemed to be considering something.

'I hope you haven't been involving young Constable

Keyse in all this investigating? I'm led to believe he's got the makings of a very fine policeman, so we don't want him to blot his copybook so early on do we, Kitty, Nora?'

'Absolutely not,' replied Kitty, answering the second question and studiously avoiding the first. She was inwardly alarmed and pleased in equal measure at how effortlessly she lied to the Chief Constable.

Sir Charles waited.

Realising more was needed, Kitty continued with the poise of an actress. 'Jimmy, sorry Constable Keyse, has actually told us not to get involved. He's been the soul of discretion throughout and has resisted every invitation we've made to give us information.'

'Well, I'm glad to hear that at least. And honestly, two pretty young women like you, don't you think you should stop all this detective work and start looking to settle down soon? Give John here some grandchildren. Let James Keyse alone and perhaps spend a bit more time with your own sort.'

Nora swallowed hard but her face remained neutral.

'Our own sort?'

'Yes, you know. Find some young gentlemen with money and prospects. I heard that Lady Atkins-Chatto's godson Raymond has just graduated from Cambridge with a first in Law. Off to the Bar and no mistake, then he's got aspirations for Parliament, clever boy.

'And what about the Lord Lieutenant's nephew Ernest? Been to Eton and Oxford, and now hoping to go into estate management here in Devonshire. And he's got a Lagonda. What do you think about that?'

He didn't wait for a reply.

'Why not invite them over for tennis before the season

ends? Nothing like fresh air, athletic endeavour and barley water to bring socially matched young people together.'

Kitty's smile was as equally fixed as her sister's.

'Thank you for the recommendations, Sir Charles. We'll certainly bear it in mind,' said Kitty, who couldn't think of anything she would like less.

*

It was just before midnight as John, Kitty and Nora walked back down the front path at Glencoe towards home, having said their final goodnights to Sir Charles, thanked him for his entertaining hospitality and asked him not to forget to pass on their gratitude to Miss Davey for her most excellent dinner.

As soon as they were outside and the door had been firmly shut, John took off his bowtie and stuffed it unceremoniously in his jacket pocket. He removed the front collar stud with an appreciative sigh and ran a comforting finger around the itchy red skin on his neck. He made a note to himself to remind Mrs Lockhart to be a little less heavy handed with the starch next time.

They stopped at the gate.

'We really are sorry papa for disobeying you,' said Kitty, laying her head briefly on his shoulder. 'Truly sorry papa,' Nora added, taking his arm and squeezing it tightly.

'As you should be, but what's done is done. Even if you constantly disobey me, ignore everything I say and your methods are somewhat unconventional, I'm proud of you for thinking you could try to save this young man's life.'

John allowed himself a brief thought about Private Parker.

They left Glencoe and walked the few yards towards home.

'But promise me one thing,' John said, looking serious for a moment.

Kitty and Nora looked back at him apprehensively.

'Promise me neither of you will seriously consider marrying Raymond-thingy-me-bob or Ernest-whatsit? They both sound utterly ghastly.'

Kitty and Nora laughed. 'I'd sooner marry Jimmy,' Kitty joked over her shoulder, opening the gate as they walked in single file up the path to their front door.

*

As they were getting undressed, Kitty suddenly stopped and looked at Nora.

'Oh Lord, we forgot to tell Sir Charles about the heel plate!'

'I remembered and decided not to,' replied Nora with a smile. 'But let's keep that to ourselves for the time being. Doesn't the defence always hold a little nugget back to flourish at the prosecution just when they think they've won the argument and all hope for the accused is lost?'

20

An arrest is made

Saturday turned out to be the hottest day of the summer.

Kitty and Nora woke later than usual, slightly feeling the effects of Sir Charles's generous measures of port, and the blueness of the sky hurt their eyes as they threw back the curtains in their room.

Mrs Lockhart had announced when she brought in the breakfast dishes that it would be cold beef and salad for dinner, and sandwiches for lunch. She put a tureen of sausages down next to the scrambled eggs and waved at her hot face with her tea towel. *I'm not cooking again today otherwise I might well pass out and bang my head on the floor, and that'll be the end of me and then where would you all be?*

If the Markhams had hoped for the usual cooling effect of the sea breeze they were to be disappointed. Even with the French windows in the dining room propped fully open the day, which had started still and airless, looked as if it had every intention of staying that way. Kitty and Nora had a few chores to do in the morning but agreed, as the heat intensified, that they would spend the afternoon in the swimming pool. It seemed the only logical option for some respite from the heat.

John didn't have a surgery on a Saturday morning but he still attended to his chronic patients or those who needed some weekly treatment, enjoying the leisurely walk around Wellesmead.

Changing dressings, monitoring blood pressure, checking up on new babies. Sometimes he dropped in for a chat and a cup of tea with one of his older, lonely patients, stopping on some mythical medical pretence or other, knowing in his heart that a few minutes of company was as good as most of his medicines.

This Saturday, he planned on going to see the Choates as well. He had been embarrassed, but also quietly flattered, that they had decided to call their new twins John, after him, and Florence after Mrs Pruitt the midwife. The two babies were thriving, which was extremely pleasing to see given their reluctance to come into the world in the first place.

He told Kitty and Nora, before he left, that if he had time when he came back he'd come over to join them at the pool.

Since Caroline's death, John had spent less time enjoying the water than he had before. When his daughters were little, he had enjoyed nothing more than spending a sunny Saturday afternoon teaching them to swim, Caroline offering words of encouragement as they floundered and splashed.

When they became stronger, John taught them the different strokes and was delighted to see they were nearly as much water babies as he was. *Doesn't seem right living by the sea and having your own swimming pool and not being able to swim*, he used to say.

Neither of them had ever managed to beat him in a straight end to end race, but Nora wasn't far off in front crawl and he suspected Kitty, with her long legs and arms and superior reach, would quite easily pass him in the backstroke now.

Today, he could see how despondent the girls were. Listless and unenthusiastic, which was very unlike them, both of them picking at their breakfast with absolutely no interest. He had to stop himself from saying, *Kitty, Nora, eat your food or don't eat your food, but stop pushing it around the plate like that.*

They had smiled wanly when he said he would come to the pool later but, despite knowing how competitive they were, he wasn't sure the prospect of racing their father, an all too rare an occurrence now, had alleviated whatever blue mood they were both obviously in.

If truth be told, Kitty and Nora were utterly deflated and downhearted after their conversation with Sir Charles at Glencoe the night before.

They felt certain they had put forward a compelling case but, despite their father's support, none of it seemed to have moved Sir Charles one iota from his belief that he was right. On reflection, they could not shake the feeling that, while they had won the battle, they had most assuredly lost the war.

After the promised sandwich lunch, they got changed and went out to the swimming pool, pulling the sleeper loungers, the small bistro table and wire chairs under a large umbrella.

They spent a good thirty minutes in the water, even

managing to laugh a little while Kitty tried to beat Nora in the crawl, unsuccessfully, until the last race when Nora had graciously given her a five yard head start.

When they got out of the pool, they sat in the sun for a little while until the heat drove them back undercover. As they dripped water onto the grass, their unhappy mood returned without much prompting.

'I really thought we had done enough Kitty,' said Nora, pulling at a piece of cotton on the leg of her bathing suit.

'Don't do that Nora, it might unravel,' chided Kitty distractedly.

'But how can Sir Charles not have thought we'd at least introduced enough doubt for him to have second thoughts?'

'I imagine getting Sir Charles to change his mind now would be a pretty tall order,' conceded Kitty. 'I can't see it happening unless someone else came forward clutching the pearls and made a full confession.'

'Yes, and that would just be too embarrassing for him to countenance. I think he'd still find a way of implicating William, somehow. Even if he couldn't pin the murder on him, he'd want the full force of the law to come down on him for the silver plate, especially considering his criminal history. You can't stake your reputation, and the reputation of your force, on something and then be seen to have been utterly and completely wrong, can you?'

'I suppose not. Oh look, there's papa.'

They both turned slightly on their seats to see John walking slowly across the lawn in their direction. He was bare legged and bare footed, a rather fetching pair of blue swimming trunks just visible under the hem of the short towelling robe he kept for swimming.

He was carrying a tray with three glasses and a pitcher on it. It looked heavy and awkward, and he groaned with relief as he put it down on the table.

'Mrs Lockhart and Norris are having a lie down in the dark so I thought I'd bring this out. Nothing like ice cold Pimms on a hot summer's day, is there? Now, how's it going? Who's up?'

'Me of course,' gloated Nora, but not unkindly to her sister. 'Four races out of five, and that's only because I gave Kitty a huge head start the last time.'

'Ha, don't get too big for your breeches, Eleanora Clara Markham. Come on Kitty, let's show her who's still the boss in the water,' said John as he started to take off his robe. Neither Kitty nor Nora made any attempt to get up. John slipped his robe back on over his shoulders and sat down on one of the wire chairs.

'All right, let's hear it. I presume these long faces of yours are something to do with last night?'

Kitty let out a long sigh, glad to be given the opportunity to vent. 'It's just so unfair, papa. We've worked really hard this week, and Sir Charles just didn't want to listen to any of it.'

'Well, to be fair to Sir Charles, he does have a lot of experience. I know you think you put forward a good case, and you really did, but he has to look at it with his policeman's head on. What will the jury believe? The real one I mean, twelve good men and true. Not just me and I'm probably biased anyway. Some of the doubts you raised were valid, but I suspect he just knows that they could all be refuted easily by the prosecution.'

'Papa,' remonstrated Kitty. 'Don't be such a chauvinist otherwise you'll be no better than Sir Charles. You know women have been allowed on juries for ten years now. Just as well, if you ask me. And anyway, we still think William is innocent.'

John reached over and took Kitty's hand. 'I know, my love, and you may be right. But sometimes being right isn't enough. Innocent men die and guilty men live, good men suffer and bad men go free, and that's just life.'

'I don't like life like that if it's so unfair,' exclaimed Nora.

'Me neither,' agreed Kitty.

All three looked up as a flash of dark blue caught their eye.

Running across the lawn towards them in full uniform was Jimmy.

He flung himself down into a spare chair and took off his helmet. He ran one hand through his hair, the blond waves sticky with sweat. His face was an alarming shade of puce and he was breathing so heavily he was not sure he would be able to speak.

'Oh, my goodness, Jimmy, have you just been running in this heat?'

He nodded.

Nora poured him some Pimms and handed him the glass. He downed it in one, belching a little from the bubbles and wiping his hand appreciatively over his mouth. He seemed to have got his breath back.

'You'll never guess what!'

'What?'

'You'll never guess,' he repeated.

Nora looked slightly exasperated. 'Hmm, let's see. They've discovered a man on the moon? A farmer on Dartmoor has captured a puma? You're going to have to give us a clue, Jimmy, otherwise we're going to be here all day!'

Jimmy looked at Dr Markham, instantly realising his enthusiasm for getting to Laburnum Villas as quickly as possible to tell Kitty and Nora what he knew hadn't taken account of the possibility that Dr Markham would be there.

Kitty saw the glance he gave her father.

'Oh, don't worry about papa,' she said. 'He knows what we've been doing this week, all except the bit about you being involved obviously.'

'Kitty!' exclaimed John, with more than a little exasperation in his voice. 'I'm genuinely concerned about what consummate liars you two are becoming.'

'Father, how dare you!' retorted Nora with mock indignation, although a small smile pulled at either side of her lips. 'It's not lying. It's just being economical with the truth under very specific circumstances.'

'So, Jimmy,' pressed Kitty. 'Spill the beans if it's not the man in the moon or puma thing.'

Jimmy took a deep breath.

'Frank Fogwill's been arrested!'

All three Markhams sat bolt upright simultaneously, as if they had been joined together by a piece of string that had been yanked up unceremoniously by an invisible puppeteer.

'What do you mean, Frank Fogwill's been arrested?!'

'I'm not sure I can be much more specific Kitty. What part of 'Frank Fogwill's been arrested' is tripping you up?'

Nora took a deep breath. 'Right, Jimmy, you'd better start at the beginning, and slowly now.'

'Can I have some more Pimms? I *am* off duty.'

Kitty handed him her half-drunk glass in exchange for his empty one. He put it down on the table and struggled out of his tunic, wafting the damp patches under his arms with relief.

'I was in the station this morning, just doing a bit of paperwork before going out on my beat when Sergeant Temple got a telephone call. I didn't hear what was being said, just him saying *Yes, Of course, Right away*, and that kind of thing. As soon as he puts the receiver down, he picks it up and calls Constable McAndrews and then Sergeant Pell. No explanation, just *get yourselves here now*. Ten minutes later they both arrive and all three have a little huddled conversation in the corner.'

Kitty interrupted. 'Couldn't you hear what was being said?'

'No, I didn't want to make it too obvious, did I? Anyway, Sergeant Temple and Constable McAndrews left and Sergeant Pell took over in custody. So when they've gone, I ask him what was that all about?'

'And what did he say?'

'Nothing much, just someone had asked for two experienced officers to go down to The Ketch Inn to speak with Frank Fogwill about Miss Watcombe's murder. Nothing specific, just put out some feelers. Find out what he knew. I didn't think much about it at the time. Seemed a bit odd but I presumed they were just trying to fill in a few gaps in their information.

'I went out on my beat and then thought I'd pop back at lunchtime to get my sandwiches. When it's hot like this, I like to take them and eat them under the oak in the square.'

'Yes, yes, Jimmy, we know,' said Kitty, failing to hide her impatience. 'Then what?'

'I arrived back just as Frank Fogwill was being dragged into custody!

'There was quite a crowd gathering outside. He was shouting and hollering about not being involved, he was an innocent man, that sort of thing. He was making such a racket that I was told to come in, put the closed sign on the door and lock it until they'd got him safely inside and the crowd had dispersed.

'They took him down to the cells and, when it was quiet again, I made Sergeant Pell, Sergeant Temple and Constable McAndrews a cup of tea. They looked like they could do with it after all that ruckus.'

'So what had happened at the inn?' asked John, intrigued despite himself.

'They'd started asking him a few questions, easy stuff. Where were you on the night of the murder? Had you ever fallen out with Miss Watcombe? Sergeant Temple said they then upped the ante a bit, put the thumbscrews on him so to speak. I'm pretty sure they didn't mean literally. They said he was starting to look uncomfortable and a bit shifty, when guess who arrived at the inn?'

'Who?'

'You'll never guess!'

'Jimmy!'

'Sir Charles! On his day off too, and just away to some fancy luncheon at the Jockey Club and then off to a box at the races. Dressed up to the nines by all accounts. Said he'd heard about the men coming to interview Frank and had decided to offer his assistance as he was passing.'

Kitty and Nora were speechless, and even John had the good grace to look somewhat incredulous at the thought of Sir Charles *just passing* such a low drinking establishment as The Ketch Inn. Given its location, the idea seemed bordering on the absurd.

'Constable McAndrews said Sir Charles was magnificent. He sent all the early drinkers outside and made Frank sit on a chair in the middle of the room. Walked around him quite menacingly by all accounts. Asked him where he was on the night of the murder, asked him about his criminal activities, asked him to account for reports of him living above his means. Frank got very nervous at this point and started shaking and almost crying.'

Kitty, still stunned, was pensive. 'I imagine I'd cry as well if Sir Charles was raining a lot of questions down on me.'

'And then what?' asked John.

'Sir Charles told Sergeant Temple and Constable McAndrews to search the place. Top to bottom. No stone unturned.

'Apparently, Frank tried to get up to protest but Sir Charles shoved him back down so hard one of the chair legs cracked!'

'And?'

'And that's when they found it.'

'Found what?'

'The pearl.'

'The pearl?'

'What pearl?'

'One of Miss Watcombe's pearls, silly. Temple found it on the floor behind the bar, wedged in between the bottom of the spirit cupboard and a broken piece of skirting board. They reckon Frank must have dropped it when he was cutting up the pearls ready to pass them onto a fence.'

'Fence?'

Jimmy couldn't help looking a little smug. 'Comes from the word Defence I believe. The defence of passing stolen goods on to a third party so a thief isn't caught with them in his possession.'

Kitty and Nora sat back in their chairs, trying to digest this development.

Jimmy continued. 'It's all over the station, so I thought I'd better get here quick as I could after my shift to let you know.

'Better still. Sir Charles made the arrest, put the handcuffs on him and everything. Dragged him out of the inn through a waiting crowd. Honestly, nothing stays secret for very long around here.

'There were fishermen, some tourists from the far end, even the press. Flashes going off left, right and centre. I imagine it'll be all over the papers tomorrow.'

'Has Frank admitted it?'

'Of course not. Even with such overwhelming evidence. Unless they think Edna did it, and that's not likely!'

'Perhaps it was one of Edna's pearls?' suggested Kitty.

'It wasn't. In between the wailing and '*no, not my Frank!*' they asked her if she owned any pearls. Of course she didn't, not even paste ones, and certainly nothing of that quality. Constable McAndrews had it in his pocket when he got back to the station. It's a beauty and no mistake.

'They think now that, in all likelihood, the pair of them were in it together. William committed the murder and Frank stole the pearls.'

'Is Frank still in your cells?' asked John.

'No, they didn't want him side-by-side with Neck for too long, concocting some sort of mutual alibi. They got him processed and quickly shipped him over to Brixham for holding.'

'Do you know what they've charged him with Jimmy?'

'Not sure but I think accomplice to murder, theft, handling stolen goods. I'd be surprised if he sees the light of day again for a good twenty years, even if he escapes the drop alongside William.'

Despite his initial excitement, Jimmy looked a bit downcast.

'I'm sorry Kitty, I'm sorry Nora. I know we all thought William didn't do it but, now the pearls have been found – well one at least – all those little anomalies we thought we'd uncovered seem to have been resolved. We knew William didn't have the pearls and now we know why. They were with Frank all along. Sergeant Temple thinks any doubt the jury might have had will now have been blown away. Easy for the prosecution to paint a compelling picture of how the two of them had planned and committed the crime together.'

'Except nothing can explain why William kept the bloody knife, or the missing gloves, or anything else?' said Nora.

John patted his younger daughter's hand. 'You can't have everything Nora. Might be he just panicked. Perhaps the fire took hold more quickly than he thought and he had to leave. Perhaps he just thought no one would look in his coat pocket in all the confusion, and he'd have plenty of time to retrieve it and dispose of it properly later. And perhaps Sir Charles was right, he just threw the gloves over the side of the pier.'

'I'm still disappointed that we were so wrong about William though,' said Kitty with a long sigh.

'Me too,' agreed Nora.

They sat in silence for a long moment, lost in thought.

'Right, let's swim,' exclaimed John, taking off his robe. 'Take your minds off it. Jimmy, I can lend you some trunks if you like. Cool you down a bit.'

Jimmy stood up. 'Thanks Dr Markham, but I'd better be off. I've already missed the bus and my mum'll be wondering where I am.'

'Can I drive you home?' asked Kitty.

'No thanks Kitty. Kind of you to offer but I'll go to the top of Smugglers' Cove Road and catch the 49. It's a bit further to walk but gets me closer to home. I'll try to pop over if there are any developments.'

They watched as Jimmy disappeared around the corner of the house.

'No more glum faces you two. Eight lengths, and I'll give you a fighting chance. You can swim it in a relay.'

21

The telephone rings twice

Nora put a piece of toast on a side plate and poured herself a cup of tea, and then picked up the Wellesmead and Barnswood Examiner. She scanned the front page before turning it around to show her father and Kitty. She turned it back so she could read out loud.

Clarence Clapp, Senior Reporter:

SECOND ARREST IN MURDER MOST FOUL!!
SIGNIFICANT EVIDENCE FOUND SAYS CHIEF CONSTABLE!

Yesterday afternoon, at approximately 1.25 pm, Mr Francis Fogwill, landlord and publican at The Ketch Inn, Smugglers' Cove Road, Wellesmead, Torquay was arrested in connection with the recent terrible murder of Miss Agnes Watcombe of Rockcliffe House in the same locale.

In a surprising twist, the arrest was made by Chief Constable Sir Charles Westacott himself. On learning of some new intelligence that had been recently received from an unnamed source, the Chief Constable had arrived unexpectedly at the location to assist his brave men.

On exiting the premises and handing the prisoner over to his Sergeants, the Chief Constable said:

'I have for some time suspected that the accused murderer, William Neck, being of low intelligence, had an accomplice in this heinous act and I'm delighted that my instinct has been proved correct.

'I can confirm that significant, and damning evidence, has been found in the possession of this known criminal.'

It is our understanding that Fogwill has vehemently denied any wrongdoing but will be charged with a number of offences, including receiving stolen goods and being the known accomplice to a murder. The prisoner has been transported for temporary confinement at Brixham.

More details inside this special issue of your Wellesmead and Barnswood Examiner.

Nora turned the paper round again so they could both take a closer look at the photograph.

It took up nearly all of the front page and showed Sir Charles, elegant and imposing, in black waistcoat, striped trousers and a *four in hand* knotted silk tie, leading Frank Fogwill out of the inn by his handcuffs.

While Frank's face was contorted and his brow furrowed, Kitty and Nora were not sure they had ever seen such a big smile on Sir Charles's face. It easily stretched from ear to ear, making his large grey moustache point upward towards his temples and bristle magnificently with his own self-importance. Slightly behind Sir Charles, a stony-faced but resolute Sergeant could be seen manfully juggling the additional apparel vital for a man of the Chief Constable's standing on his way to the Jockey Club; his grey top hat with the black silk band, his cane, his kid gloves, his binoculars.

A large caption under the photograph proclaimed:

He's got his man!!

'I see the exclamation marks are proliferating,' said John under his breath.

Nora tossed the newspaper down in disgust.

'For some time I've thought the murderer had an accomplice,' she mocked. 'What absolute piffle! Sir Charles hadn't even thought about that until we mentioned all the other potential suspects.'

'He certainly looks like the cat that's just got the cream, doesn't he?' Kitty added, reaching over for the paper.

'Nice photograph though. Very *Sir Charles* if you know what I mean! I imagine as we speak he's on the phone to the newspaper to order a print, large as he can get. Probably already planning where he's going to hang it at Glencoe, somewhere prominent no doubt. Perhaps over the front door so you can't avoid it!'

'Girls, look on the bright side. You may not have convinced Sir Charles about William but you did give him some food for thought about Frank. Put him under the spotlight a bit more than he had been and at least the mystery of the pearls has been solved.'

'But why do we still feel so terrible?' asked Kitty, and Nora nodded in agreement.

'We wanted to save one man from the gallows and now we might have sent another one there!'

John stood up, folding his napkin neatly.

'Disappointment. It's a hard emotion to swallow but one you'll have to get used to, especially if you want to continue with this silly investigation work. Sometimes, the person finding the lost purse doesn't hand it in, they steal it, and the poor cat that goes missing doesn't get returned home safely, it gets run over by a train. This has been a good life lesson Nora, Kitty. Take the successes where you can and put the failures behind you.'

Nora shook her head slightly, trying to get the image of a flattened Horus out of her mind.

'Papa, I don't think you can equate finding a lost cat to failing to save a man's life,' said Kitty.

'I know my darling.' John kissed both his daughters as he did every morning. 'But you and Nora will just have to try the best you can to come to terms with it.'

*

After their father left the dining room, Kitty and Nora ate in silence, both lost in their own thoughts. Mrs Lockhart had burned the toast and the only sounds were the old grandfather clock in the corner as it ticked and Nora scraping ash onto her plate.

The door opened and Mrs Lockhart put her head into the room.

'Kitty, telephone for you.'

'Oh, thanks Lockie, did they say who?'

'No, just a woman's voice. Sounded quite cultured.'

With a quick quizzical glance, Kitty drained her teacup and Nora swallowed down the last corner of burned toast.

Mrs Lockhart started to gather up the tureens, but Nora placed her hand on Mrs Lockhart's arm and stopped her.

'Don't worry, Lockie, we'll bring those through in a moment. Best get back to the kitchen.'

Trying not to feel as if she was being invisibly rushed out of the room, Mrs Lockhart turned with a sigh and left.

Kitty counted to ten, and then the twins rushed into the hallway. Kitty picked up the phone, holding it slightly away from her ear so that Nora could lean in and hear too.

'Hello, this is Kitty Markham.'

'Oh, hello Kitty, it's Jean. Jean Carmody.'

'Hello Jean, how nice to hear from you.'

'I can't talk for long. I only have a few pennies and there are two people already waiting outside the booth.'

'Of course, I understand. How can I help you?'

'I've just seen the newspaper about Frank Fogwill being arrested. What terrible news! I know he and Miss Watcombe hadn't always seen eye to eye but he was so kind and generous to her, it's almost inconceivable that he was involved.'

There was a pause, but Jean continued just as Kitty wondered if the line had disconnected.

'I thought you'd like to know. I went to the police station on Friday. I had a message that they are taking William over to Exeter tomorrow and they asked if I wanted to come and collect his possessions as they don't have the room to store them any longer.'

Jean hesitated before continuing. 'They gave me a big box of some of his clothing and, well, I found his gloves.'

'Where were they?'

'They were actually tucked down low in the inside pocket of his jacket. I remember he sometimes kept them there when he was out working in the garden, in case he needed to pull up a spikey weed or something similar. They were rolled into a tight ball and you would hardly know they were there. I wanted to get his jacket cleaned ready for when he comes home,' she added and Kitty thought she heard Jean's voice catch slightly.

'I checked his gloves and I thought you'd like to know, there was no blood on them, inside or out. I was a nurse before I went into service and I could tell they were completely clean. Is that any use to you?'

'I'm sorry Jean, I don't think it is. We've reached the end of the road with our investigation I think. But please, do keep them wrapped somewhere, and perhaps find a way of giving them to William's counsel when he's appointed. It might help at trial, inject a bit of doubt if you know what I mean, even if it is only for one juror it might be enough.'

'Thank you, I hadn't thought of that. I'll keep them safely to one side.'

'Thank you for calling Jean, it was useful information.'

There was another pause.

'Actually, that wasn't the main reason I called.'

'Oh?'

'Yes, something quite strange has happened. When I picked up the box of William's things, the nice Sergeant at the station said they'd also put the silver plate into the box, you know, the one William is supposed to have stolen. I didn't think anything of it and then yesterday, while I was unpacking the last few items, I saw it. They had kindly wrapped it in a piece of cloth to protect it, but I thought I'd take it out and polish it ready for when I get allowed back into the house.'

'Yes?'

'It didn't belong to Miss Watcombe.'

'Pardon?'

'No, it didn't belong to Miss Watcombe. I've never seen it before.'

'Are you sure?'

'Positive. I know all Miss Watcombe's silver intimately. You can't clean something every two weeks for nearly fifteen years without knowing that this wasn't hers.

'To be honest, I'd always wondered how William was supposed to get hold of a piece of her silver in the first place. She always kept the silver cabinet locked, religious about it she was. I had a key and she had a key. I don't know where she kept hers but I imagine it was safely hidden away and I'm sure mine never left my side.'

'How can you be sure it wasn't one of her pieces?'

'Well, it has a rather attractive design engraved on it, sort of stylised flowers. Believe me, I have never seen it before in my life. What do you think I should do? Shall I keep it and let William's counsel know, along with the gloves?'

Kitty looked at Nora who hunched her shoulders, *no idea but how suspicious!*

'Absolutely. Keep them both safe. I know we said there wasn't anything else we could do but we've still got a whole day. We'll see if we can make some more enquiries. It definitely seems very odd indeed.'

'Thank you, Kitty, that's so kind of you. I've got to go, goodbye.'

'Goodbye,' replied Kitty, but the line was already dead.

She gently put the receiver back in its cradle.

'The plot thickens Nora, the plot thickens.'

*

Kitty and Nora walked back to the dining room to collect the crockery and cutlery and were just inside the door when the telephone rang again.

A harassed looking Mrs Lockhart came bustling out of the kitchen, drying her hands on her apron. 'It's like Piccadilly Telephone Exchange in here today!' she exclaimed, picking up the receiver. 'Wellesmead 839.'

There was silence as she listened.

'Yes, I told you, this is Wellesmead 839, but there's no one called Edie Dearlove at this address.'

Nora covered the twenty feet from the dining room to the telephone in two seconds, rather unceremoniously snatching the receiver from the hand of a startled Mrs Lockhart. She covered the mouthpiece as she passed it to Kitty who wasn't far behind her.

'Don't worry, Lockie,' Nora said, spinning Mrs Lockhart around and walking her back towards the kitchen. 'It's for Kitty. Some amateur dramatics thing she's doing. All very exciting but a bit hush hush, we don't want father knowing until she gets the part.'

Mrs Lockhart looked heavenward, and tutted, her face saying, *you Markham girls will be the death of me.*

Once Mrs Lockhart was safely ensconced in her kitchen, Nora returned and, as before, they held the receiver close, their temples almost touching.

'Hello, sorry, have I got the wrong number? I'm after a Miss Edie Dearlove.'

'Yes, sorry, this is Edie Dearlove. That was my landlady you just spoke to, I'm new here.'

'Ah, not a problem Miss. It's Sergeant Pell at Wellesmead Police Station. Do you remember me?'

'Yes Sergeant I do. How are you?'

'Well thank you Miss. Prisoner Neck has asked me to call you.'

'Oh yes.'

'He's made a formal request for you to visit him today, and I was ringing to see if you would be available at any point.'

Unbeknown to most people, Sergeant Andrew Pell was a man of faith who, despite that, did not believe in the concept of an eye for an eye although that was a view he kept strictly to himself. He knew he would be mercilessly ribbed by his colleagues for being such a wet fish if they realised he had an optimistic view of human nature and a strong belief that meant, however hard he tried to condemn any guilty man, he could not quite bring himself to think any human being had the right to take another's life. That was the prerogative of God and no one else.

Sergeant Pell had taken a bit of a shine to young Neck over the few days he had been in his care. He seemed polite, calm, reasonable to deal with. Always said please and thank you. He wondered if there was a nice lad under the hard criminal exterior.

Sergeant Pell knew Neck would be leaving Wellesmead tomorrow and, given what everyone was saying at the station, the chances of him ever seeing freedom again, or even life, were vanishingly small. The thought of his impending trial and inevitable execution troubled Sergeant Pell greatly.

If Neck wanted to see his young sweetheart one last time, what was the harm? No one would be any the wiser and at least Sergeant Pell would feel like he'd done some little good in the world.

'Of course, Sergeant, I'm free all day. How kind of you to let me come and see my William one last time.' Kitty dry sniffed, hoping to inject some emotion into her performance. 'Would eleven be suitable?'

'Ideal Miss. I'm afraid I can only give you five minutes again, like last time.'

'I totally understand Sergeant Pell. Thank you so much for calling. I'll be there at eleven.'

22

The condemned man receives a visitor

Kitty reached into the back of the wardrobe for the old clothes she had worn last time, but they were creased and unwearable. Cursing herself for not taking the time to hang them up, she found a plain dark blue dress, unfancy and simple. It looked a little more expensive than she thought Edie Dearlove might wear, but not so couture that it might arouse any suspicions with the Sergeant.

She found the old brown beret and tucked it into her handbag.

Nora said she would stay at home and keep their father and Lockie occupied if they happened to be wandering around aimlessly. Hardly likely, she knew, especially for their father as he had a full surgery list that morning but he might just decide to stretch his legs between patients.

As Kitty turned the corner away from the house and

towards the High Street, she scrubbed her lipstick off with a tissue and carelessly shoved her hair under the hat. It still felt slightly damp from the last time she had worn it but it was too late to change her mind now. As she passed Froggitt's window at the farthest end of the little row of shops from the police station, she stopped for a moment to check her reflection.

Good, perfectly nondescript she thought, *and every inch Edie Dearlove.*

The station was quiet and Sergeant Pell looked up as the little bell above the door tinkled to announce a visitor.

His face lit up with recognition.

'Good morning, Miss Dearlove.'

'Good morning, Sergeant, I'm sorry I'm a little bit early.'

He glanced at the clock. Ten fifty-two.

'Not at all. Now, I don't have any spare constables here today to chaperone you. I can come down and let you in to William's cell but I'll have to lock you in I'm afraid. I can't be away from the counter for more than a minute. I hope that is suitable?'

Kitty swallowed, quelling a little frisson of anxiety at the thought of being confined with a man that everyone said had the capacity to slit the throat of a defenceless old woman without a second thought. She crossed imaginary fingers in her head, *I hope you're right about him, Kitty!*

Sergeant Pell fixed Kitty with a stern look.

'I'm going to trust you Miss. No funny business, do you hear me? I don't want to find out you've abused my trust and good nature and been up to anything nefarious, do I make myself perfectly clear young lady?'

Kitty nodded. 'Perfectly, Sergeant. I just want to say goodbye to my William.' She sniffed.

Seeming satisfied, Sergeant Pell lifted the hatch to the counter, skirted around Kitty and locked the outer door. He turned over the little sign from OPEN to CLOSED.

He looked at the clock again. Ten fifty-three.

'You can have until eleven o'clock, on the nose. Follow me please Miss.'

Kitty followed the sergeant down the worn steps to the cells beneath the street, waiting patiently while he unlocked and locked the outer door. It was as gloomy as she remembered, but quieter this time. There was no shouting or banging and an air of resignation seemed to have replaced the menace.

Sergeant Pell banged on William Neck's door.

'Neck, Miss Dearlove is here to see you as requested. Five minutes only. Stand away from the door.'

Checking through the bars to make sure William was not intent on making a last minute dash for freedom, Sergeant Pell unlocked the door and stood aside to let Kitty enter.

He indicated to Kitty to step in a little further so he could close the door and pulled it to with a heavy thud. Kitty jumped despite herself. She took two deep breaths as she heard the metal key scrape into the lock and turn, metal on metal. Involuntarily, she turned around to look at the locked door.

William Neck was standing by the far wall, leaning against it. The little metal table had been pulled up towards the bed and Kitty could see some playing cards laid out in a game of solitaire. An open packet of cigarettes lay on the bed, alongside a rough earthenware ashtray and a copy of the morning paper. Kitty could see just the edge of the photograph and one bushy side of Sir Charles's moustache.

'Don't worry Miss,' he said, sitting back down on the bed in front of the little table. 'I won't hurt you. I saw my sister a few days ago. She came to give me a few shillings so I could have some creature comforts until they haul me off. She said you were still trying to help so I'm hardly going to bite the hand that feeds me, am I?'

He picked up his turned over cards and added a red two to a black three, and a black Jack to a red Queen.

'Anyway,' he added, looking back up at Kitty, 'I thought you believed I didn't kill Miss Watcombe?'

Kitty looked around the spartan little room, its depressing grey walls damp and mouldy, the sunshine above hardly penetrating the gloom except for a rectangular sliver that almost perfectly illuminated the table and William's playing cards.

'I do. We don't have long William. Is there something you needed to tell me?'

William indicated to the chair, and Kitty pulled it up on the opposite side of the small table.

'Please, take a seat. This won't take long,' he said, and Kitty sat down.

Despite being in the middle of a game, William swept all the laid out playing cards into his open hand, squared them off and put them down at the bottom of the bed.

'I know who Jean's fella is,' he said, his round eyes holding Kitty's.

'Who?'

William picked up the paper and refolded the edges so only the photograph was visible.

He put it down on the table in front of Kitty and indicated with his finger.

Kitty looked confused.

'What, that sergeant is Jean's lover?'

'No idea. I know him of course, that's Sergeant Temple. He was the one who was with us when we went into the house and found the body, but I never saw him at the house before then.'

'So how do you know it's him?'

'I recognise the cane.'

Kitty looked closer at the photograph. He was right, you could see the top of the cane Sergeant Temple was holding as he juggled the paraphernalia that Sir Charles had undoubtedly passed to him so his hands would be free to parade Frank Fogwill outside for everyone to see.

'But that's an elephant not a bird?' Kitty said, frowning. 'Look, here are its ears and its trunk.'

William smiled and reached out. He slowly rotated the newspaper so that the photograph was facing him and away from Kitty.

She looked again, a little closer this time, and her heart did a slow, sickening lurch, sinking to the pit of her stomach before rising back up like bile, blocking her lungs so she felt like she couldn't breathe.

Upside down, the elephant's face no longer looked like an elephant's face.

The trunk was now the long slender neck of a swan, the curled tip its head and beak and the flapping ears perfectly formed wings.

William's forefinger tapped at the photograph.

'That's the cane I saw in the hall stand. The one with the swan on it,' he said simply.

23

The truth will out

Kitty walked as fast as she could away from the police station and towards home, her head down and, all the while, trying to process the information she had just learned from William Neck.

It seemed wild, preposterous almost, that Sir Charles had anything to do with the crime even if, by some slim chance, William was not mistaken and the cane had belonged to Sir Charles and, thus, he was Jean Carmody's lover.

As she rounded the corner towards Laburnum Villas, Kitty saw Nora standing by the gate, and they waved. Nora's ready smile disappeared almost instantly as she saw the look on Kitty's face.

'Quick,' said Kitty, taking off the beret and putting it back in her handbag. 'We need to see Jean Carmody. I'll explain on the way.'

They rushed into the waiting room of their father's surgery. Mrs Carmichael was just making an appointment on the telephone and two people were waiting quietly and patiently in the small space.

'Mrs Carmichael,' whispered Kitty as quietly as she could. 'Can we please go in to see our father, it's very important.'

Mrs Carmichael frowned.

'He's with a patient Kitty,' she replied, glancing at her watch. 'He should only be another minute or two, can you wait? I'm sure he wouldn't mind if you just went in after they've come out, but only for a moment. He's running slightly late and he already has other patients waiting,' she said, indicating the two figures seated in the waiting room.

Thankfully for Nora and Kitty, almost immediately the door to their father's consulting room opened and an elderly gentleman came out.

Not noticing his daughters, John put his head around the door.

'Mr Armitage,' he said but, as one of the patients rose, he spotted Kitty and Nora.

'Oh, hello you two,' he said rather surprised. It was unheard of for him to see them on a Monday morning while he was working. 'To what do I owe this unexpected pleasure?' As Nora's had done two minutes previously, his smile died as he saw Kitty's worried face.

'Can we come in to see you father?' Kitty said. 'Honestly, we'll only be one minute.' She looked at her father's next patient who had resumed his seat with a barely audible tut. 'I'm so sorry Mr Armitage, we won't be long. Two shakes of a lambs tail, promise.'

Once inside the consulting room, John closed the door behind them. 'Whatever's the matter Kitty? Are you ill? You look terribly pale.'

'No, I'm fine. Can Nora and I borrow Betty?'

'Now?'

'Yes now.'

'Whatever for?'

Kitty and Nora exchanged glances. 'I can't tell you, we just need to pop out. We'll have her back within the hour.'

John shook his head, a feeling of concern washing over him although he was not sure why.

'Of course, but come and tell me what this is all about when you get home.

'Drive safely,' he added, but Kitty and Nora had already left, slamming the door behind them.

*

Kitty drove carefully, as she always did, albeit a little faster than normal, all the while telling Nora about her conversation with William.

Nora's reaction was what Kitty would have expected, the questions tumbling out.

'Kitty, he must be mistaken!'

'Are you sure that's what he said?'

'Can we trust his recollection?'

'Seems unlikely, don't you think?'

They reached Seaview Parade in Brixham and Kitty brought the car to an abrupt halt outside number seventy-eight.

Without waiting, they half ran up the little path and rang the door bell.

Jean Carmody opened the door, unable to hide her surprise.

'Oh, hello Kitty, Nora. How nice to see you both.'

'Can we come in please Jean?'

'Of course. Come on through. My, whatever's the matter Kitty? You don't look well. Can I get you a glass of water?'

'No, I'm fine thank you. We just need to ask you something and it's quite urgent.'

They sat down in the little rear sitting room as they had done last time they visited. Kitty took a deep breath.

'I've just come from the police station. I went to see William.'

Jean Carmody sat up straighter, a look of surprise on her face.

'Whatever for?'

'He got the sergeant there to call me. He said he had something important to tell me.'

'Oh, what was it?'

Kitty took another deep breath, but this was not a time for protecting anyone's sensibilities.

'He told me he recognised the cane of the man who is your lover. He saw it in the newspaper.'

Out of the corner of her eye, Kitty could see a neatly folded copy of the morning paper on the sofa next to Jean.

'Is Sir Charles Westacott your lover?'

There was a long silence. Jean Carmody looked at her fingers which were knotted together in her lap.

She looked up. 'Yes.'

Nora let out an audible sound, blowing out her cheeks.

'Why on earth didn't you tell us?'

'As I told you before, it was irrelevant to your investigations and certainly to William's case. Sir Charles is clearly above reproach.'

'Jean, no one is above reproach, certainly not when a murder is being investigated,' implored Kitty.

Jean Carmody shook her head in disbelief. 'You aren't honestly saying you think he was involved in some way, do you?'

'We don't know but it's really, really important that you are honest with us now Jean. Your brother's life could depend on it!'

'Of course. I don't suppose it matters now but, whatever you think of me or Charles, I can guarantee that the relationship that he and I had, are having, is not relevant. So, go ahead, what questions do you have for me?'

'Do you know if Sir Charles knew Miss Watcombe while she was alive?'

'Well of course he did,' replied Jean. 'They had been great friends from the time he was a young policeman and she had come back from India. They'd even been part of some philanthropic society well before the war. It's where Miss Watcombe became such a passionate advocate for prison rehabilitation. It was a cause she and Charles shared.'

'Did he ever come to Rockcliffe House before you became romantically involved?'

'Only once that I remember. It was her birthday and he arrived at the house out of the blue. He'd been so thoughtful, brought a cake and some lovely flowers. It's when I met him for the first time actually.'

'I'm sorry, this is a very personal question, but when did you and he start having a close relationship?' asked Nora.

Jean bristled slightly at the implication of the question but, despite her desire to object, the steely look in Nora's eyes persuaded her not to.

'It wasn't much longer after that. Perhaps a month or so later. Charles never came back to visit Miss Watcombe, he said it would have looked strange. But I bumped into him in the park on my day off and he bought me an ice-cream and we sat and chatted for a while.

'He is a lovely man, so caring, so generous. I know what we did was wrong, especially going behind Miss Watcombe's back, but I couldn't see what the harm was. I've had little happiness in my life and Charles was such a devoted friend.'

'How often did he come to the house?'

'Perhaps once or twice a month. No more. I was nervous at first, but we always chose times late in the evening, after Miss Watcombe had retired to bed, and when I knew Nelly and William would be asleep.'

Kitty tilted her head to one side.

'This is really important Jean. Do you remember if you asked Miss Watcombe about employing William, or if Sir Charles did?'

'I don't know if Charles did. I'm not sure how he could as he never visited with her after that first time. He could have written I suppose. But I know he was very pleased when I told him that I'd asked her and she had said she'd be very happy to give William a job. It was such a weight off my mind, and I knew both Miss Watcombe and Charles were dedicated to supporting offenders to find a better, more righteous path away from their past crimes.'

Jean looked more composed than she had previously.

'Is that all the questions you have? I'm very tired and thought I might take a nap so I hope you won't mind if I ask you to leave now?'

She stood up.

Kitty and Nora stood up too. They could not think of any more questions for Jean.

'Thank you, Jean, we appreciate your honesty.'

As they reached the car, Nora hesitated.

'She's right, you know? We don't have anything that links Sir Charles to the crime itself. And, what's the best we can hope for? Embarrass Sir Charles and Jean, perhaps make it difficult for him because he's lied about his association with her and Miss Watcombe?'

Kitty looked across Betty's roof at her sister.

'Wait here, there's something else I want to ask Jean.'

Nora got into the passenger side and watched her sister go back up the path. Jean Carmody opened the door, a few words were exchanged and they both went inside. No more than three minutes later, Kitty emerged and joined her sister in Betty.

'Are you all right?'

'I'm fine.'

'What did you want to ask her?'

'I wanted to see the silver plate she'd had returned from the police station.'

'And?'

'I've never seen it before in my life but I think I recognise the engraving. Jean had said it was some stylised flowers but I'm pretty sure I know what they are. They looked like Yorkshire roses!'

The sisters looked at each other, the same connection obviously being made.

'And how many people do we know here in Devonshire who are from Yorkshire?' asked Nora.

'Just one,' replied Kitty.

'Now what?' said Nora.

'Let's go and find Arthur, shall we?'

24

Death comes to Wellesmead

'It hurts like a bugger, doctor, and my Janet doesn't find it very appealing, not given where it is, if you know what I mean?'

John peeled away the edges of the dressing. The abscess was developing like a small volcano, the outer infection now much more concentrated, the skin hot and red and the white head sticking proud.

'It's looking grand Bill. Coming along nicely, just as I'd expect it to. But it's going to hurt for a few more days I'm sorry to say. It just needs to rise a bit more before I can stick a spoon in it, like a good soufflé.'

Bill Tooley had never had a soufflé and, if truth be told, he was not exactly sure what one was, but he trusted the doctor knew what he was talking about.

'I'll put a new dressing on it today and then I think, if it's convenient for you, I'll pop over next week, probably Tuesday afternoon. It should be ready to go then and you'll feel a lot better when we've got all that nasty pus out of it.'

John walked over to the little cabinet where he kept a stock of medical supplies that he used most days. Bandages, dressings, an ear syringe, tweezers and the like.

As he lent over to find the right sort of dressing for Bill Tooley's abscess, John saw Betty racing up the driveway. He flinched thinking, *slow down Kitty or you'll run into the garage doors*!

Betty came to an abrupt halt outside the garage but, instead of getting out to open the garage doors and put the car away as they always did after they'd been out, Kitty and Nora leapt out, slamming the car doors carelessly and ran back down the drive and around the corner in the direction of Glencoe.

A little shiver of alarm tingled on John's scalp. *That was odd*, he thought. He picked up the dressing and turned back to Bill.

'Okay, let the dog see the rabbit,' he quipped, finding it hard to shake the feeling that something was terribly wrong with Kitty and Nora.

The abscess and Bill appropriately dressed once more, John led him out into the waiting room and said his goodbyes. 'See you next week Bill and remember, keep it dry and tell Janet to try not to prod it.'

Mrs Carmichael had already tidied the waiting room, something she did religiously every day as soon as Dr Markham's last patient had been shown into the consulting room. The magazines were neatly stacked, the chairs wiped down, the blinds pulled.

'Is there anything else you need from me this morning, Doctor?' she asked as usual.

'Can you just put Bill Tooley in the diary for my rounds

next Tuesday afternoon? But that's it for today, thank you Eloise. See you tomorrow.'

John waited for her to write in the diary and put it back in the top drawer of her desk before she left. He turned the little sign over in the window that detailed his opening hours and locked the door.

Back in his consulting room, he looked out of the window again.

Betty was still sitting on the drive and there was no sign of Kitty or Nora.

There it was again, that almost imperceptible feeling of apprehension.

John went back into the house via the door marked 'PRIVATE' and locked it behind him as he did each day. As usual, he went straight upstairs to change his shirt but, for some reason, he hesitated before leaving his bedroom.

He opened up the doors on the large walnut wardrobe and, by stretching, he could feel the box on the top shelf, tucked back behind a hat box and Caroline's old sewing bag.

He pulled the heavy box out, balancing it carefully so as not to drop it and put it on the bed.

*

Kitty and Nora knocked as hard as they could on the front door of Glencoe and waited, fidgeting and looking around them, trying to catch their breath.

Miss Davey opened the door, her expression possibly more set than normal. Today, she looked positively grim.

'Hello Miss Davey. We're sorry to bother you but can we please see Arthur? Just for a few minutes. It's very important.'

Normally one to find any reason to obstruct the Markham sisters from consorting with Arthur, something in their faces today made Miss Davey hesitate. She had her own troubles and was in no mood to find out what was ailing Kitty and Nora.

She could not quite place their look. Worried perhaps, frightened?

'Of course, come on in and wait in the parlour.'

'Can we wait in the drawing room please?'

'If you prefer, but it's nicer in the parlour at this time of the afternoon.'

'Honestly, we'd prefer the drawing room.'

Their expressions had an edge of determination that convinced Miss Davey that they would not be persuaded, so she opened the front door slightly wider and they let themselves in.

'I'll fetch Arthur.'

As soon as the drawing room door had closed, Kitty and Nora started scanning the photographs on the wall. 'I'm sure I've seen something here before,' said Kitty. 'I wish I could remember where.'

She spotted the small photograph she had seen before, nicely framed in burr walnut.

'Here it is!' she exclaimed and Nora rushed over from the other side of the room.

Kitty read out loud. 'The Novus Initium Society Annual Dinner Dance 1900.'

'New Beginnings,' said Nora.

'What?'

'New Beginnings. It's Latin.'

They stared at the photograph. There was Sir Charles

almost in the middle, surrounded by twenty or so other smiling people, the gentlemen in dinner jackets, the ladies in evening gowns.

'There!'

Kitty pointed at one figure partly obscured by a large, bald man. An attractive woman, probably in her forties, stylishly dressed in a black silk dress with puffed sleeves. It wasn't her dress that caught Kitty and Nora's attention though. It was her necklace.

Although partially covered by the man's arm, they could see it clearly. The Mannar pearls. The woman in the photograph was a young Agnes Watcombe.

'He can't deny he knows her now, can he?' Kitty said breathlessly, taking the photograph off the wall and turning it over.

There was a small brown label on the back, peeling and torn, the lettering faded but still readable.

Kitty read out loud.

'*The members of the Novus Initium Society enjoying a night out at The Carlton, celebrating the second year of the formation of their exclusive society to support the ideals of the rehabilitation of offenders and care of prisoners.*'

They both looked up sharply as the door opened.

'Hello?' said Arthur lightly, curious about what Kitty and Nora were doing at Glencoe at this time of the day.

'Come in quickly Arthur and shut the door,' said Nora, gesturing him over. Kitty put the photograph back on the wall.

'Arthur, does your father have any silver with a pattern on it, like a stylised rose? The Yorkshire rose?'

Arthur thought for a moment. 'Sounds familiar. He does

have a few old pieces like that. I think he inherited them from his father. Why?'

'Do you think you could find a piece?'

'I know exactly where they are. They're in the sideboard cupboard in the dining room. He never uses them but that's where he keeps them. Do you want me to have a look?'

'Yes please, and hurry. If you find something like that, can you bring it back?'

'Of course.' Without any hesitation, Arthur left the room and returned less than a minute later, shutting the door quietly behind him.

'Here,' he said, handing a small bonbon dish to Nora.

'Is it the same?'

Kitty looked at the dish. 'The piece Jean has is bigger but yes, it's the same pattern all right.'

All three looked up, startled, as the drawing room door opened.

Nora instinctively put the bonbon dish behind her back and her other hand protectively on Arthur's shoulder.

'Oh, hello Sir Charles. We didn't expect you to be at home at this hour of the day,' Kitty said with as much lightness as she could muster, despite the pounding of blood in her ears. She felt her cheeks flush and hoped Sir Charles wouldn't notice.

Sir Charles was dressed for the outdoors in a navy Fairisle sweater over a white shirt and burgundy tie, tweed plus fours and long blue socks.

'I was just out to play golf, thought I'd treat myself to an afternoon off after the excitement of the last few days. Miss Davey's running around with a face like a slapped derriere and I saw Arthur sprinting down the stairs two at a time, so I thought there was a fire or something.'

He stopped and looked at Kitty, then Arthur and then Nora.

'And my, you're all looking a bit guilty. What have you broken? I hope it's nothing valuable otherwise Miss Davey will skin you alive,' he joked, but his smile died on his lips as Kitty and Nora stared at him, unmoving and unsmiling.

'Why did you tell us you didn't know Miss Watcombe?' Kitty asked.

Sir Charles's expression was fixed. He put his golfing cap down on the armoire.

Before he could answer, Nora added, 'and we know you and Jean Carmody are lovers.'

Arthur jumped in surprise.

'Arthur,' said Sir Charles sternly. 'You can leave while I talk to these young ladies.'

Arthur didn't move.

'I'd rather stay if that's all right father,' he said, feeling Nora's hand on his shoulder reassuringly grip him more tightly.

'As you wish. You're a young man now. Can't harm you to learn a few facts about how the world works.'

'So, what of it, girls?' Sir Charles said, turning to take a cigarette from the lacquered box on the armoire next to his cap. He didn't light it but concentrated on rolling it idly around in his fingers.

'You've met Jean Carmody. She's a mighty fine looking woman and I am not without my needs. I'd known Miss Watcombe a long time ago, so I don't think it would have influenced the case against Neck one way or the other if I'd admitted a previous acquaintance.'

Nora took in a deep, steady breath.

'We think you killed her.'

Arthur flinched again, but kept his eyes firmly on his father, despite an almost overwhelming desire to ask Nora to stop squeezing quite so hard.

Sir Charles laughed, a sly, rasping noise that had no humour in it.

'Is that right? I'm all ears. I can't wait to hear what evidence you've got to support that ridiculous and scurrilous accusation Nora. Kitty, what about you? I presume you think I'm a murderer too, or has your sister just taken leave of her senses?'

'No, we both think you killed her.'

'Why, because of something Jean said? Or perhaps William? I heard from Sergeant Temple yesterday that Sergeant Pell had let an attractive, if plain, young lady in to see him recently. Needless to say, he's in hot water, and I did wonder if that might have been you Kitty. Sounded awfully like you from the description I had, despite some talk of a dreadful hat.'

'You're right, it was me. We think William Neck's an innocent man and you've framed him.'

Now Sir Charles did laugh outloud, taking out his handkerchief to mop at his eyes.

'Now here's a fine turn up and no mistake. I'm not sure what hypothesis you both came up with to support this madness. Or was it Neck put that ridiculous notion in your heads? Honestly Kitty, you should know better than to listen to the lies and ramblings of the lower orders, and criminal ones at that. If either of you repeat this nonsense outside these four walls, I won't be able to protect you from being hauled in front of the court to explain yourself.

'Tampering with a witness, at the very least, possibly perverting the course of justice? Either way, it won't look good for either of you and if you think they'll believe a word that lying scoundrel has to say, you're going to be very much disappointed.'

'William didn't say anything about you being the murderer, he just pointed us to you as Jean's man friend.'

'So, is that it?'

Sir Charles put the cigarette between his full lips then took it out again, absently pulling a piece of tobacco off his lower lip.

'I agree it could be a bit sticky for me for a while, you know, having not been totally truthful about my past connection to Agnes and my present connection to Jean, but that hardly makes for compelling evidence of my guilt as the murderer, does it?'

'But this might!' said Nora, taking the bonbon dish from behind her back.

'What've you got there?'

'It's a piece of your silver service, Sir Charles. The one your father gave you, I believe. Probably unique with this Yorkshire rose pattern, I'd suggest. Strange how it matches the piece of silver found under William's bed. Jean has just shown it to Kitty so there's no point denying it. I must say though, it seemed a bit rash of you, secreting a piece of this set under William Neck's bed. You should have picked a nice piece of Meissen perhaps, or a Staffordshire dog or a nondescript silver spoon or two.'

'We know you're too arrogant to think you'd ever get caught in the first place, so who would ever know, but that was a very silly thing to have done,' said Kitty. 'Yes, very disappointing for such a master criminal,' added Nora.

'But didn't you yourself once tell us that even master criminals can be stupid?'

Nora took a half step backwards as Sir Charles came and took the dish out of her hands, putting it down carefully next to his cap.

He turned his back to take a lighter out of the drawer and Kitty allowed herself a sideways look at Nora, whose eyes were fixed rigidly on Sir Charles's back.

Sir Charles lit his cigarette and took a few deep puffs, the smoke rising above his head. He stubbed it down in the ashtray and then reached further into the drawer.

As he turned, Kitty, Nora and Arthur could see the distinctive black barrel of a gun in his hand.

'Now, that was a very stupid thing for you to do Nora. You too Kitty.' He pointed the gun in their direction.

Kitty, Nora and Arthur took an involuntary step backwards at the sight of the gun.

'What are you going to do, Sir Charles? Kill us? Kill Arthur? You'd never get away with it.'

'How melodramatic you are Kitty,' he replied. 'Let's just say I'm keeping my options open.'

'So, do you deny it?' breathed Nora.

'Of course I deny it. I'm not sure that paltry nonsense you think you've got would convict me but ....,' he hesitated, thinking about the possible consequences before continuing, '... but it might not go well for my standing in this county.

'But I'm sure an expensive King's Counsel and a little pressure on my darling Jean to say she was mistaken and showed you the wrong piece of silver would be sufficient to sway the minds of any right thinking jurors. Arthur, come over here.'

Arthur shrugged off Nora's hand and stepped in front of her and Kitty protectively.

'No father. I won't. I believe Kitty and Nora.'

'Don't be stupid boy. These two silly, silly girls have absolutely nothing to link me to the murder of poor Miss Watcombe.'

'No, but this might,' said Arthur, reaching into his pocket for his handkerchief. He took out the heel plate and held it up between his thumb and forefinger. He tilted it slightly so it caught the light.

'I found this at the scene of the crime and I can prove it was left by the murderer. It was in a pool of blood, Miss Watcombe's blood.'

Sir Charles flinched and his cheeks flushed with barely concealed anger.

'I think if you'd taken the time to check, Arthur, you would see none of my shoes are missing such an item. I can't believe you have fallen for these stupid girls' preposterous ideas!'

Kitty looked at Sir Charles. 'But I wonder if we took it down to Mr Sinclair at the cobblers and asked him if you'd been in for a repair to one of your shoes, say the day after the murder, whether or not he'd confirm it?'

'And I imagine he would say, *how odd, Sir Charles never brought his own footwear down for repair. It was one of Miss Davey's jobs. And yes, that is identical to the heel plates we use here.*'

Sir Charles let out a sigh, studying his gun as if in contemplation.

'Please stop waving that gun around Sir Charles, you're frightening us,' implored Kitty.

'So now I have two pieces of evidence to deal with. A silver plate, easy, and a heel plate, equally easy. While Sinclair might confirm everything you say Kitty, again it hardly ties me to the crime does it? Say the murderer did lose a common-or-garden heel plate at the scene, and the Chief Constable, completely coincidentally, loses a similar heel plate and decides to visit the cobbler himself while he was out in town, rather than bother his poor, hardworking housekeeper.'

Nora's shoulders dropped and she looked at Kitty. *He's right*, her look said, *he has the status and connections. No one will believe us, and everyone will believe him.*

Sir Charles visibly relaxed.

'So, if that's all the evidence you've got, I don't think we have to continue with this charade any longer, do we? Now, what to do with you three?'

A creaking sound to their right made them all look over, to see the door to the drawing room open. Miss Davey took a step into the room. She was holding a gun in her right hand, her left hand balled into a tight fist.

'They might not have enough to convict you, Sir Charles, but I think I do.'

She stepped further into the room, the gun held casually in front of her, and opened her fist.

Sitting in the centre of her palm was something round and black and shiny, the lustre catching the light. It took a moment to register, but Nora and Kitty's mouths opened almost simultaneously. One of the black Mannar pearls.

'I found it this morning while I was cleaning your study. I agree with Nora, you are awfully careless for a criminal Sir Charles. Didn't you even bother to count them when you cut them up? This was on the floor behind your desk, and it will be the thing that sees you pay for your crime.'

Movement to their left caught their attention and they

looked to see John Markham at the French doors which were ajar. He stepped inside, smiling reassuringly at his daughters and Arthur. John was also holding a black gun. He turned his head and nodded towards Miss Davey. Her face was grim but she nodded back in acknowledgement.

'Ah, if it isn't the wonderfully upstanding Dr Markham,' said Sir Charles sarcastically. 'Come to join the party, eh, John? Don't tell me, you've got some evidence too.'

John held up his gun and pointed it at Sir Charles.

'Put the gun down, Charles, you're scaring my daughters and you're scaring Arthur.'

He turned towards his daughters.

'Kitty, take Nora and Arthur out please. I don't want you to stop and wait, run straight to the house and lock the doors tightly. I'll be there as soon as I can.'

Without hesitation, Kitty took Arthur's hand and Nora led the way out of the open French doors. Normally ones to find fault with their father's logic or question him endlessly, this time they left without a word.

They walked as far as the gate and then ran as quickly as they could back to Laburnum Villas.

25

Only one possible verdict

WITNESS TESTIMONY
WITNESS TESTIMONY (Taken by Chief Inspector Maurice Lowndes, Metropolitan Police)	
ML	Please state your full name for the records.
JM	John Robert Markham.
ML	Were you present in the Drawing Room at 'Glencoe' in Wellesmead, Torquay on the afternoon of Monday 4th August 1930 at approximately 1.30 pm?
JM	Yes.
ML	Who else was present in the room at that time?
JM	Miss Constance Davey and Sir Charles Westacott.
ML	Can you tell me in your own words what happened?
JM	Yes. Sir Charles Westacott had a gun and had been threatening my daughters, Catherine and Eleanora Markham, and his son Arthur Westacott.
ML	Where were the Misses Markham and Master Westacott at the time of the incident?
JM	I had told them to return to Laburnum Villas and wait for me there.

ML	Why did you go to Glencoe at that time?
JM	I had seen my daughters from my surgery window approximately ten minutes before. They were walking in the direction of Glencoe and they looked concerned, so I thought I should go and investigate.
ML	Did you take a gun with you?
JM	Yes, my old service revolver, a Webley.
ML	It is our understanding Dr Markham that your gun was rusted and unusable, suggesting it had not been fired for many years. We also confirmed there were no bullets in the gun. Is that correct?
JM	Yes. I don't think it has ever been fired.
ML	So why did you take it?
JM	I am not sure. I thought my children might be in danger. Father's intuition, I suppose.
ML	But your gun would not have been of any use, would it?
JM	No. Perhaps I thought it would be a deterrent.
ML	Did you observe Miss Davey holding a gun?
JM	Yes.
ML	Do you know what sort?
JM	I didn't see it clearly and all those old service revolvers look the same, but I suspect a Webley too.
ML	And is it right that Sir Charles Westacott's gun was also a Webley?
JM	I believe so.

ML	A single shot was heard at approximately 1.40pm. Can you account for the six minutes between the time of the shot and your telephone call to Dr. Arbuthnot, which he recorded as 1.46pm?
JM	No, I can't specifically account for it. I think both Miss Davey and I were in shock and I was probably consoling her. I also spent some time trying to assess Sir Charles's condition and revive him, although it soon became clear that he was deceased.
ML	Can you speculate why Sir Charles Westacott may have wanted to take his own life?
JM	My daughters have been investigating the recent murder of Miss Agnes Watcombe and believed that the suspect William Neck had not committed the crime. I understand they also had uncovered some evidence to suggest Sir Charles's involvement.
ML	Did you see Sir Charles put the gun towards his head and pull the trigger?
JM	Yes.
ML	Did he say anything before he pulled the trigger?
JM	No.
ML	Is there anything else you would like to add?
JM	No.

WITNESS TESTIMONY
(Taken by Chief Inspector Maurice Lowndes, Metropolitan Police)

ML	Please state your full name for the records.
CD	Constance Evelyn Maes-Davey.
ML	Were you present in the Drawing Room at 'Glencoe' in Wellesmead, Torquay on the afternoon of Monday 4th August 1930 at approximately 1.30 pm?
CD	Yes.
ML	Who else was present in the room at that time?
CD	Dr John Markham and Sir Charles Westacott.
ML	In your own words, can you tell me what happened?
CD	Yes. Sir Charles Westacott had a gun and had been threatening Dr Markham's daughters, Catherine and Eleanora Markham, and his son Arthur Westacott.
ML	Where were the Misses Markham and Master Westacott at the time of the incident?
CD	When Dr Markham arrived, he told them to return to Laburnum Villas and wait for him there.
ML	Why were you in the room at that time?
CD	I had let the two Miss Markhams into the drawing room, and knew Master Arthur was also present. When I heard a commotion, I went in and saw Sir Charles pointing a gun at them.
ML	What sort of commotion?
CD	Raised voices.
ML	Did you take a gun with you?

CD	Yes.
ML	Where did you get the gun?
CD	I'd rather not say but it was given to me during the war.
ML	So why did you take it into the room?
CD	I am not exactly sure. I had that day discovered some evidence that implicated Sir Charles in a terrible crime and I thought I might need the gun to protect myself.
ML	It is our understanding that your gun is fully serviced and serviceable, and had six bullets remaining in it at the time of the incident. Is that correct?
CD	Yes.
ML	Why do you keep your gun active?
CD	Habit I think. As I said, it has always been a comfort to me for protection, given the sorts of people you may encounter.
ML	Did Dr Markham have a gun?
CD	Yes, a Webley I believe.
ML	And is it right that Sir Charles Westacott's gun was also a Webley, and that your gun was also a Webley?
CD	Yes.
ML	Can you speculate why Sir Charles Westacott may have wanted to take his own life?

CD	The two Markham sisters and Master Arthur had just confronted him with some evidence of his involvement in the murder of Miss Agnes Watcombe. I heard this through the door before I entered. I then presented my own evidence. I think he realised that the evidence against him was overwhelming. Sir Charles Westacott was a man who, above all else, valued his status and position in the community and county. I truly believe he wouldn't have been able to live with the shame and ignominy, or face the hangman, if we had been proved correct.
ML	Did you see Sir Charles put the gun towards his head and pull the trigger?
CD	Yes.
ML	Did he say anything before he pulled the trigger?
CD	No.
ML	Is there anything else you would like to add?
CD	No.

Wellesmead and Barnswood Examiner
Friday 8th August 1930

TORQUAY – Suicide

An inquest was held on Thursday 7th August 1930 at The Wellesmead Community Hall in the presence of Dr Sir Albert Moxhay QC DFC, Coroner for the county of Devonshire, the facts of the case being as stated below.

On Monday 4th August 1930, at approximately 1.50pm, the body of the Chief Constable of Devonshire, Sir Charles Westacott, was discovered in the drawing room at his home, 'Glencoe,' Wellesmead, Torquay by Dr David Arbuthnot of Marchhaven.

Dr Arbuthnot had been telephoned shortly before that time by Dr John Markham of Laburnum Villas, Wellesmead, Torquay. Dr Markham said a man had been shot and an independent doctor was required. Dr Arbuthnot made his way at speed to 'Glencoe'.

On arrival at the scene, Dr Arbuthnot observed both Dr Markham, and Miss Constance Davey, housekeeper, in the vicinity of a male lying on the floor, at that time yet to be formally identified.

Dr Arbuthnot assessed the victim and confirmed the prone man was dead. Dr Arbuthnot noted a single gunshot wound to the front of the head of the deceased, consistent with a small pistol or revolver.

While the positioning of the entry wound seemed somewhat awkward, Dr Arbuthnot had no hesitation in concluding it was a self-inflicted gunshot wound, supported by the corroborating accounts he received at the scene by the two people present at the time of the incident, namely Miss Davey and Dr Markham.

Police later confirmed they had recovered a Webley pistol from the scene, believed to belong to Sir Charles Westacott. It contained five bullets and one spent casing, the conclusion being that the fired bullet was the one that had killed Sir Charles.

In conclusion, the jury had no hesitation in returning a verdict of suicide.

In his summing up, Dr Sir Albert Moxhay, QC DFC stated:

"This is a terribly sad end for a man who was, until this time, well respected within the community and had risen to hold extremely high public office through his own merits. I am aware that both Miss Davey and Dr Markham have provided statements to the police which have given identical accounts of the incident, and I do not feel the need to burden them further by asking them to recount the details of this horrendous act here. Needless to say, they are both of outstanding and faultless character and it is fortunate that two such upstanding members of our community were present to attest to the last known act of Sir Charles Westacott.

Given the gravity of the accusations against Sir Charles Westacott, and the public interest, I would like to put on record my sincerest thanks to the Metropolitan Police of London for making themselves available at short notice to conduct interviews with all relevant parties and to take over the investigation of the alleged crime.

Further to my personal conversation with the Commissioner, I understand that Sir Charles Westacott is now the only suspect in the murder of Miss Agnes Watcombe of Rockcliffe House, and that all the evidence gathered to support this terrible fact will allow everyone who has been caught up in his web of deceit and lies to draw a veil over this most heinous and saddening of crimes."

26

Means, motive and opportunity

Jimmy spied John Markham in one of the flower beds, wielding a trowel without much enthusiasm, and walked over to greet him.

'You need to get yourself a full time gardener, Dr Markham,' said Jimmy.

'Hello Jimmy,' replied John, standing up and flexing his tired muscles.

His knee popped. 'Did you hear that? I'm getting too old for all this bending and stretching. I'll have to see if I can persuade Willie to do a few more hours, these hydrangeas are starting to get away from me.'

'Are Kitty and Nora here?'

'No, they're not back from Jean's yet. Hopefully soon.' John looked at Jimmy's duffle bag.

'Come prepared for swimming?'

'Yes, if that's all right? I bumped into Nora at the station. She was just leaving after giving her statement to that Chief

Inspector Lowndes and she said come over for a swim after my shift if I had time.'

'Jolly good idea.'

John surveyed the overgrown shrubs critically, flexing his back. 'I think I might join you.'

'Excellent. May I just go up and change?'

'Of course, you know where. I'll be up in a minute.'

John and Jimmy spent an enjoyable half hour in the pool, both competitive but, as with Kitty and Nora, John having the upper hand in all strokes.

'Gosh, that's tiring, but you've almost got me beaten on that backstroke, Jimmy,' said John, hitching himself out of the water to sit on the grass. 'Do you fancy a beer? I think there are some cold bottles in the pantry, I hide them from your auntie behind the bottled plums.'

'Oh, yes please.'

Jimmy sat on the edge, his feet dangling in the water, and a few minutes later John reappeared with two brown bottles, already opened. He handed one to Jimmy and they both took an appreciative swig.

As they sat in companionable silence, they heard the sound of a car engine. They could not see the driveway from the pool, but the sound got louder, tyres on gravel signalling the return of Betty. Then there was silence.

Minutes later, Kitty and Nora walked across the lawn to the pool.

'Hello you two,' said Nora. 'I'm not sure alcohol and cold water mix very well papa, I thought you'd know that.'

'Well, luckily for us, we've done our swimming. Call this a much deserved post-competition treat.'

'How did it go?' asked Jimmy.

'I think we'll go and get changed first, come on Nora.'

They turned to leave. 'Oh, papa,' said Kitty over her shoulder, 'can we have a beer too? Just this once? We're both absolutely parched. Betty does get unbelievably hot.' Nora nodded enthusiastically in agreement.

A few minutes later, Kitty and Nora returned, Kitty in her navy blue bathing suit with the white piping, Nora in shocking pink with yellow daisies on the straps. Kitty dropped her beach bag onto the grass, and pulled out two pairs of sunglasses, handing one pair to Nora.

John had gone back into the pantry and retrieved four more bottles of beer, and they pulled the sleeper seats and the wire chairs under the umbrella.

He handed another beer to Jimmy, and then one to each of his daughters. 'If you see Mrs Lockhart, hide these. We'll never hear the end of it if she catches you swigging out of a bottle like two common navvies.'

'So?' asked Jimmy, struggling and failing to hide his impatience.

Kitty sighed.

'Well, Jean is devastated as you can imagine. She truly loved Sir Charles and she believed with all her heart that he felt the same way about her.'

'Charles fooled a lot of us for a long time Kitty. I hope you told her she wasn't the only one?' said John with a resigned shrug.

'Of course, but I'm not sure how much it helped, especially after what she's learnt about him.'

'Have the police been to see her?'

'Yes, they went over on Friday. They gave her the two pearls, the one Miss Davey found and the one Sir Charles planted on Frank.'

'Doesn't that seem a bit odd?' said John, looking up from his beer.

'Not at all, said Kitty. 'Because guess what? They found Miss Watcombe's will in Sir Charles's papers. Looks like Sir Charles stole it on the night of the murder.'

'Why would he do that?'

'Probably because he knew Miss Watcombe was leaving the house and all her worldly possessions to Jean. We'll never know for sure but he probably wanted to further inveigle himself into Jean's affections before the will was discovered. He didn't dare risk looking like he was only really interested in Jean for her money.'

Nora nodded in agreement. 'I suspect after all the furore had died down, he would have found a way to slip the will back into Miss Watcombe's papers. Make it just look like his useless officers had missed it in the search.'

John raised his eyebrows in surprise. 'Ah, so the pearls and everything else are now legally Jean's. Well, I never!'

They sat in silence for a moment.

'Oh, how is Frank, does anyone know?' asked John.

'I saw him yesterday actually,' said Jimmy. 'He's had a bit of a fright as you can imagine. I think Edna aged twenty years since last week and that's not a pretty thought. But, he's a tough cookie is our Frank.

'I'm sure, when he's got over the shock of being accused of something so terrible, he'll be dining out on the story for the next ten years. He said he's even going to get a copy of the photograph that was on the front of the paper, you know, the one with him being arrested, and put it over the bar.'

'And what about Nelly?'

'Ah yes, poor Nelly,' continued Jimmy. 'Ed made her go

into the police station and tell them that she'd made up the whole story about seeing William put the silver plate under his bed. Apparently, it was her own idea, nothing to do with Ed at all. When she heard about the police finding a silver plate and William being arrested, she thought she'd be protecting Ed if she said she'd seen William hide it. Actually, it was Ed who made her confess to the police about lying all along. Seems like he's not such a bad lad after all.

'I think Sergeant Temple gave her a serious lecture and sent her home with a flea in her ear.'

'I think it's a lesson to us all,' said Nora. 'Never judge any book by its cover.'

'Do they know how he did it, I mean how Sir Charles planted the pearl in The Ketch?' asked Kitty.

'They're not sure, but probably in all the confusion, he just dropped it and kicked it. Risky, but what else could he do? Luckily for him, it ended up where it did. The game would have been up there and then if it had ricocheted off the bar and landed back at his feet.

'I suspect he was worried about the missing pearls casting doubt in any juror's mind about William's guilt,' added Jimmy.

Nora pulled a face. 'I'm afraid I think that was probably down to us.' Kitty and John nodded in agreement. 'We thought the missing pearls might somehow help William's case and we told Sir Charles.'

John nodded. 'Looking back, it did all seem a bit coincidental that Sir Charles unexpectedly turned up and then they found the pearl in The Ketch the day after we'd had dinner at Glencoe.'

'Jean said the police had also given her the diamond, ruby and emerald clasp from the pearls. They found it in Sir

Charles's nightstand. She said she might have it made into a brooch, a little reminder of Miss Watcombe.'

'Any theories from your lot on where the rest of the pearls ended up, Jimmy?'

'No, but long gone by all accounts. Sir Charles was massively in debt apparently. They found papers and betting slips in his desk alongside the will, and a little book detailing all the people he owed money to.'

'We always knew he was a racing fanatic, but I had no idea he was such a gambler,' John added.

Jimmy nodded. 'Turns out he'd gamble on anything. Horses, dogs, football. Anything and everything. I got the impression he was in hock for a huge amount.'

'If he needed money, why didn't he just stop sending Arthur to that fancy school? That must have been costing him a fortune.'

'That's not something a man like Sir Charles would have contemplated,' said John. 'His status, his standing in the county, that was his ultimate power. He would never have done anything to suggest that he was having financial problems.'

Jimmy took a sip of beer.

'They found some other papers locked in Sir Charles's desk. Letters he wrote to Miss Watcombe, and her letters to him. He must have stolen his back at the same time as the will. Seems when Miss Watcombe returned from India, she and Sir Charles had an affair. He was much younger than her of course but they met at the Novus Initium Society. There doesn't seem to be any indication it lasted long, but from what was written, it looks like she was still quite smitten with him.'

'What a monster!' exclaimed Kitty. 'Duping two poor innocent women like that.'

'Yes, an absolute cad,' added Nora.

'He probably went round to Rockcliffe House to inveigle his way back into her affections and then met Jean. Perhaps Miss Watcombe told him that day over tea how much she valued Jean and how she was leaving her everything when she passed. I imagine someone like Sir Charles, with such an insatiable greed, realised he could do so much better than just persuading Miss Watcombe to give him a few hundred pounds.'

Kitty pondered this for a moment.

'Yes, it does seem likely now, doesn't it? Jean says she met Sir Charles again in the park sometime after he'd been at the house and it now all seems terribly staged. Convince Jean that he was in love with her, murder Miss Watcombe, steal the pearls to fill the gap in his debts, wait a decent amount of time and then marry Jean and have the house and all the money she'd been left in the will.'

'What a bastard!' Jimmy muttered under his breath. 'Oh, sorry Kitty, Nora.'

'I just don't know how someone could be that devious?' sighed John, shaking his head.

'Oh, it's much worse than that,' replied Jimmy. 'In one of his letters, he reminds Miss Watcombe of their interest in prisoner rehabilitation from back in the day. He'd learned from Jean that William was due to get out of prison soon, so it didn't take much for him to plant the seed in Miss Watcombe's head that the charitable thing to do would be to offer him a job.'

'Ah, so as soon as she did, Sir Charles knew he had the

perfect stooge to pin the murder on,' said Nora, nodding as the realisation came to her.

Jimmy continued. 'It was actually very easy. Jean told him she was going to be away that night, and he certainly didn't want to do anything to endanger her life at this stage. He was lucky again. Apparently, she'd also said that William was going fishing that evening so Sir Charles probably thought he had the place to himself except for Nelly, and her quarters were at the other end of the house. Turns out William was actually just drinking down by the pier so was on hand when he saw the flames. By all accounts, he was actually quite brave, getting the axe and trying to cut back the timbers to stop the fire.

'Given how conscious Miss Watcombe was about security, and thinking there was no one else at home, she wouldn't have opened the door to a stranger, but she obviously let Sir Charles in. Maybe she thought this was some prelude to him rekindling the relationship they'd had so long ago.'

'Poor, poor Miss Watcombe. She didn't see what was coming, did she?'

'Probably not. Sir Charles likely hit her with a piece of firewood before slashing her throat. It was then easy enough to drop the bloody knife into William's overcoat pocket and put the silver plate that he had brought with him under William's bed.'

'Poor Miss Watcombe and poor Jean,' agreed Kitty and they sat for a few moments, thinking about the two women who had been so cruelly used by Sir Charles.

'Does Jean know what she's going to do now that she's an heiress?' asked John.

'Well, I don't think there was quite as much money as

Sir Charles must have been hoping for, but enough so she'll be comfortable. She says she's going to sell what remains of the house to Frank. Sort of payback for all his troubles, I suppose, assuage her guilt a bit.'

'I don't see what she has to feel guilty about,' said John.

'She thinks if she'd told us sooner we might have saved him getting caught up in Sir Charles's scheme but who knows?' said Nora with a shrug.

'Anyway, Frank is going to demolish the rest of the house and build some holiday chalets,' added Jimmy. 'Sees himself as the king of the holiday-makers I suspect. He says it's the future. He'll turn the rest into that car park he always wanted, get more wealthy people driving down to The Ketch.'

'Jean and her sister Emma are then thinking of moving away,' added Nora. 'They've got their eyes on a little Bed and Breakfast up in Llandudno. Some place a long way from here and the memories.'

'And the gossips,' added Kitty. 'She's an innocent in all this, just like Miss Watcombe, and William, and Frank, but mud sticks doesn't it?'

'And what about William?' asked John. 'Has Jean heard from him since he was released?'

'Yes, he was at the house this morning,' said Kitty with a broad smile.

'And he gave Kitty such an enormous hug, I thought he was going to pop her ribs!' declared Nora.

'How is he?'

'Shaken I think. He's had a rough start in life but he wants to begin afresh and we absolutely believe he will. Jean is going to give him some money and he says he fancies going to Canada of all places, trying his hand in the timber business. Maybe even buy a little yard up in Saskatchewan or Manitoba.'

'I'm pleased for him,' said John, the face of Private Parker swimming vaguely into view.

John studied his daughters.

'So with all this good news, why do you both look so glum? You look like you've lost a shilling and found a penny.'

'I was just thinking what terrible detectives we are,' said Nora, her mouth turned down in a little moue of dismay. 'We missed so many things along the way. We should have been more persuasive with Jean about her lover, and we fell into the same trap as everyone else. Believing only a criminal like William could have committed the crime, and not someone like Sir Charles.'

'I was thinking about poor Arthur,' said Kitty. 'We're pleased that we've saved William of course but, whatever sort of monster Sir Charles was, he was still Arthur's father.'

John raised his eyes.

'I've been meaning to tell you. I've been contacted by the Westacott's solicitors asking me to attend the reading of Sir Charles's will. Miss Davey and I are going along to support Arthur but we aren't worried about him,' said John with a broad smile, 'he's a sensible, resilient little chap.

'And despite everything, Kitty, Nora, I'm proud of you both and your maman would have been proud of you too. Although, I do have to say, I'm perhaps not so happy with your methods and certainly not of putting yourself into such terrible danger. You saved an innocent man,' he said simply, adding silently to himself '... *something I failed to achieve.*'

As if finally happy to acknowledge their achievement, they all lent forward in unison and clinked their bottles.

'Oh, William gave me this to say thank you,' said Kitty, putting her beer back on the table. She reached into her beach bag and pulled out a beautifully crafted corn dolly. 'He's very artistic, he made this with some straw he pulled out of his mattress in the cell. Isn't it lovely?'

'Sergeant Pell won't be pleased when he finds all the stuffing missing.'

'How is he? I feel terribly guilty that he got into trouble for letting me into the police cells.'

'Don't worry about Sergeant Pell. He's had his wrist slapped but he's far too good an officer for there to be any lasting damage.'

'Oh, and something else!' added Nora, asking Kitty for the bag.

She reached inside and brought out her handkerchief. She tipped the contents into her hand and lent forward, opening her fingers to reveal the two pearls, one black, one white.

'Jean wanted us to have these. She said it would be nice as a reminder of what we've achieved. We thought we'd use some of our savings to have them made into two pendants, the black pearl for Kitty and the white one for me, if that's all right papa?'

'I can't think of anything nicer,' agreed John.

27

Where there's a will

Since the incident, Arthur had been living at Glencoe, just him and Miss Davey.

They had locked the drawing room, neither of them wanting to go inside it after the death of Sir Charles but, when he was asleep one night, Miss Davey had gone in and rolled up the rug which still had a dark stain on it and put it out for the rubbish collection.

She had also taken down all the photographs and asked Arthur if he wanted to keep them but he said he didn't.

Arthur still had two photographs of Sir Charles and his mother when they were first married, laughing and hugging in the garden of Glencoe, a very young Arthur standing between them, smiling broadly, the outline of the house just visible behind them. That was the only memory he wanted to keep, happier times.

His father's solicitors, Kingsley, Gerard & Knowles, had been in contact with him soon after hearing about the death. They had read the will to Arthur in their offices, John Markham and Miss Davey at his side for moral support.

Mr Kingsley, the senior partner, had lowered his glasses to the tip of his nose and read slowly.

'This is the last Will and Testament of Sir Charles Jermain Westacott of Glencoe, Wellesmead, Torquay.'

'Then there's some legal jargon I won't bother you with Arthur, but it's very short anyway.'

'I, Sir Charles Jermain Westacott, being of sound mind, leave all my worldly possessions, estate and property, both real and personal, to my son by adoption, Arthur Westacott (formerly Parminter) with the exception of an annual stipend of £1,000 per annum to my housekeeper Miss Constance Davey of the same address.'

Mr Kinglsey lowered his glasses and pinched the bridge of his nose.

'In reality, we are probably only talking about some personal items. Sir Charles was not solvent financially apart from the bricks and mortar asset he had in Glencoe.'

And what about Sir Charles's debts?' asked John Markham.

'Luckily for Arthur, his father's gambling debts aren't enforceable so he's under no obligation to settle them.'

Arthur had looked up. 'But I want to pay them,' he said simply.

Mr Kingsley looked through his folder of papers, having gathered a number of documents from Sir Charles's desk at Glencoe.

'I'm afraid Arthur that is a considerable amount, running into several thousand pounds. There is no way you could do that without selling Glencoe.'

'I'll sell Glencoe then. Will there be enough to pay Miss Davey?'

'Yes, the house is worth quite a substantial amount I believe, it's certainly one of the biggest properties in Wellesmead. I don't think there would be enough for you to continue at Charlton but certainly enough for a small monthly amount for living expenses and the residue could go into a small trust fund which should give you a modest return when you are twenty-one.'

Miss Davey stood up. 'Thank you, Arthur, that's very kind of you, but I would rather not take any of Sir Charles's money. You have it all.'

Despite Arthur's subsequent protestations over the next few days, Miss Davey was not one to be dissuaded easily. However, after some cajoling, the occasional tantrum and a few tears, mostly from Arthur, she had eventually acquiesced and agreed to £100 only, just enough she said to get settled into a new position and have a small nest egg for her future.

'But only because you've asked me Arthur,' she said.

28

Partners in crime

'Guess what?' said Arthur. 'Miss Davey told me a secret.'

There was silence.

'Well, don't you want to know what it was?'

'I think the point of secrets Arthur,' replied Kitty, 'is that they're secret.'

Kitty, Nora and Arthur were walking Norris on the Green.

The weather had started to turn, the summer evenings shortening and the heat dissipating to a gentle September warmth, a hint of autumnal chill in the freshening breeze blowing off the sea. Soon it would be dark by teatime, the tennis net would be put away and the pool left to fill with leaves as it did each year in the winter before they made it useable again the following spring.

Arthur reached down to scratch Norris behind the ear, which he seemed to enjoy. Mrs Lockhart, knowing in her heart it was the right thing to do, had been stricter with Norris for the last month, resisting his pleading whines for plate scrapings and even, on occasion, taking him for a walk herself to the end of the road and back. While he may not have appreciated it, he was certainly starting to look surprisingly trim.

'Oh, Miss Davey wouldn't mind me telling you two.'

He lent in a little closer. Nora looked around at the Green, the large grass area empty except for the three friends and Norris. Nora smiled at him.

'I don't think there's anyone listening Arthur!'

'When she was younger, Miss Davey was in the Belgian resistance in Antwerp.'

He paused for some dramatic effect, pleased by the surprised look on Nora and Kitty's faces.

'Well I never!' said Nora.

'She told me she used to do all sorts of amazing things. She'd gather intelligence, helped run an underground paper, even set up a clandestine postal network. But her main job was helping captured resistance members to escape. Isn't that thrilling?'

Kitty thought about Miss Davey. So serious, so rigid, so impenetrable. All those whispered rumours about her being a spy or working in military intelligence now didn't seem quite so fanciful after all.

'Very. Just like all those novels by John Buchan you love so much Arthur.'

'Didn't Sir Charles tell us once he'd served in Antwerp during the war?' asked Nora. 'One of the top jobs in Command I think.'

'Yes, I think he did. I wonder if he and Miss Davey knew each other then?'

'I don't think so,' said Arthur. 'I'm sure they would have said something, being on the same side and all that.'

It had been nearly six weeks since the incident in the drawing room at Glencoe.

In the immediate aftermath of Sir Charles's death, there had been a whirlwind of interest, not just in Wellesmead but nationally as well. It wasn't every day someone of Sir Charles's importance and social standing was unveiled as a corrupt policeman, a cold-hearted murderer, would-be embezzler, philanderer and inveterate gambler.

The local paper had enjoyed several continuous days of salacious headlines and lurid details, and more exclamation marks than Dr Markham could cope with.

He had threatened to cancel his subscription so, since then, Mrs Lockhart had kept the local newspaper in the kitchen for her and his daughters to read, and only put The Times on the sideboard in the dining room for Dr Markham to enjoy over his breakfast.

Kitty and Nora had both been invited to the police station to give their statements to the Metropolitan Police and hand over the evidence they had uncovered, as had Jean and Jimmy. In the end, the only reasonable conclusion the investigators could come to was to agree with everything Kitty and Nora already knew.

There was talk of a police commendation, the sisters foisted into the spotlight, demands for interviews, magazine articles, even a fashion shoot, but Dr Markham was having none of it. 'This isn't a time for celebration,' he said and, for once, they could not disagree with him.

'Anyway Arthur,' asked Kitty, 'how is Miss Davey? She looked remarkably well last time I saw her.'

'Quite chipper I'd say.'

Nora bent down to pick a buttercup. 'For a woman who'd

just seen a man kill himself, she seems to have recovered from the ordeal remarkably well. Oh, sorry Arthur.'

'It's all right. I don't mind talking about it.'

'Has she packed?'

'Yes, almost ready to go. Off on the night boat next Thursday, then on the train to Paris. She said she may stay there for a few days and then go up to Liège to look for a post. She has some distant family there I think she said.'

'I didn't even know her mother was Belgian before this, did you?' asked Kitty.

'No, she never did share much about herself.'

'Did she take the money in the end?'

'Well not what she was entitled to but I made her take £100, that's all she wanted.'

'I wonder why she didn't want more?'

'I don't know. She deserved it and I know my father would have wanted her to be provided for, that's why he put it in his will, but she was adamant and there was just no persuading her.'

'And you can't argue with the Belgian resistance, can you?' said Nora with a small smile.

'When do they think the sale of the house will go through?'

'Not sure, probably next month. They say it's a dentist and his family come down from Edinburgh. They sounded nice.'

'And at least if father gets any patients with toothache, he won't have far to send them,' added Kitty.

Nora looked pensive for a while.

'Let's hope they're extremely boring and dull.'

'We can but hope,' agreed Kitty. 'And what about you Arthur, what will you do?'

'Miss Davey thinks I should move away from here. She's worried that the stigma of being the son of a murderer will stay with me for a long time.'

'But you don't care what other people think, do you?'

'I don't think so.'

Kitty, Nora and Arthur walked along in silence for a few minutes, Norris even finding the energy to chase a couple of seagulls that had landed on the grass looking for worms.

Kitty and Nora couldn't hide their genuine sadness that Arthur was not going to be living next door to them in a few short weeks.

'It'll be so odd not to have you there, Arthur,' said Nora with a frown. 'Who will we pass notes to now?'

'Yes, and what if we want someone to climb a tree, or get into a tight space, who can we call on then?' added Kitty.

'Where do you think you'll go?' asked Nora.

Arthur shrugged, kicking idly at a clump of tussocky grass.

'I don't know yet. My mother had an aunt who lives in Scarborough, so I might go there. I'll need to find a job though. I'm sort of wishing I'd listened to my father more. He may have been a cold-hearted murderer, but he did try to get me to study. I'm just not sure what I'm going to be able to do.'

'I have an idea,' said Nora.

She told them her plan and Kitty and Arthur smiled in agreement.

'No guarantees,' she added, 'but definitely worth a try.'

*

John Markham was in his study, tidying up some papers.

He concentrated hard on the menial task, finding it

helped his mind not wander back to the events at Glencoe. He had seen violent death so many times that it hadn't affected him as much as he had thought it might. It was knowing that his daughters had been in danger that made him feel a cold sweat break out down his spine. It was too awful to contemplate what could have happened.

There was a soft rapping on the door, and he looked up from his receipts.

'Come in.'

Kitty stepped inside, closely followed by Nora.

'Hello, you two. I was just thinking about you. Do you fancy a spot of lunch? I thought we could walk down to the harbour. Mrs Lockhart says there's a new café opened. Does quite nice battered cod I hear.'

'That'd be lovely, thank you papa, but can we ask you something first?'

John frowned. Experience had taught him that when he had the fleeting thought that his daughters were just about to gang up on him, they usually did.

'Of course, what is it?'

They walked over to his desk, side by side, hands behind their backs, obviously well-rehearsed in what they were about to say.

'You know Arthur?'

'Of course I know Arthur, what a strange thing to ask Kitty.'

'You know Miss Davey's leaving for Belgium next week, don't you?'

'Yes.'

'And the new family from Edinburgh are moving into Glencoe the week after next?'

'Yes, I heard.'

'Arthur will be homeless then. He doesn't have any close family so he's going to have to go and live with his great-aunt in Scarborough.'

'Well, Scarborough's lovely. Your mother and I went up along that North East coast for our honeymoon. Very pretty.'

'But it's so far away and Arthur wants to stay here in Devonshire.'

'And?'

'He won't be going back to boarding school, there isn't enough money for it and you know he hated most of it anyway. But he was exceptionally good at chemistry. Remember when he built that baking soda and vinegar volcano?'

'How could I forget?'

John clearly recalled the mess on the nice clean paving at the side of Laburnum Villas all too well.

'Anyway, we wondered if he could come and live here with us? We've got oodles of space. He can pay his living expenses of course and we thought he might be able to do some sort of apprenticeship with Hester. Dispensary Assistant or Medicines Auditing Junior, or the like. He'd be in his element.'

'No pun intended,' added Nora somewhat unnecessarily.

'You know how busy it's getting in there. So many more medicines to prepare, lotions and potions, creams for this, pills for that. And you know how much Hester wants to do her pharmacy exams. She'd really appreciate having another pair of hands in the dispensary.'

John sat back in his leather chair, rocking it on the feet, his fingers forming a tent to his lips, as if in serious contemplation.

'I suppose it could work, but maybe Arthur wouldn't want to live here given everything that's happened?'

He could see Kitty and Nora starting to smile. They've won me round, he thought to himself. *Hard to say no to them given that I was already going to make that same suggestion*, he thought, although he had to admit the idea about the apprenticeship was an excellent one.

'We've already asked him and he'd love to,' said Kitty brightly.

'And, just think papa,' added Nora. 'It'll help redress the balance a bit for you. You always used to complain about how outnumbered you were by women in this family, and Norris doesn't really count. It'll be nice for you to have another man around the house, and Arthur wouldn't have to pretend to like listening to the cricket on the wireless like we do!'

'If I say yes, I have one stipulation,' said John, trying to affect a serious expression.

'Anything.'

'No more detective work. I know the temptation will be almost overwhelming with Arthur here, and Jimmy at your beck and call, but I don't want to hear any more about you two running around the district looking for puzzles and mysteries to solve. What you've just been through is quite enough to last you both a lifetime.'

'Of course not,' said Kitty.

'Absolutely not,' agreed Nora.

The side of Kitty's left hand touched the right side of Nora's. They were sure their father wouldn't be able to see their crossed fingers from where he was sitting.

8421 Chausser d'Antoine
Liège
Belgium
29th December 1930

My dearest Dr Markham

Thank you so much for your Christmas card. It was most thoughtful of you. Thank you also for asking about my new position. I am happy to confirm that Madame LeMenier is a most generous employer.

Arthur writes often and has told me of your kindness to him. I am delighted that he has found a vocation in life that he actually enjoys, and I know he thinks of you as a sincere and decent mentor in lieu of any father of his own.

While I know we agreed we would never speak of it again, I feel I must write with regard to the incident that binds us together. I know that you are a man of integrity so I hope, in time, you will see that your discretion that afternoon was the best result for all concerned. I was able to right a terrible wrong from a much darker time, one that I had carried in my heart for many years. As I told you, I had only become aware of the terrible connection I had with Sir Charles in recent years and I regret, until that day, I had not found the courage I needed to act.

The knowledge that his cruelty had extended over many years, and the thought of poor Miss Watcombe in her final moments, gave me the courage I had not been able to find for so long. In the end, John, we must never let evil flourish unchecked and consequences must always be paid, regardless of the passage of time.

Despite everything that transpired, I pray every night that Sir Charles will rest in peace but, while doing so, will have an eternity to ask forgiveness for his sins, all of them.

I wish you and your wonderful daughters much peace, health and happiness.

They have a unique talent. Remind them every day to be brave, even when they sometimes falter.

With seasons greetings and lasting gratitude.

Constance Maes-Davey

Hi, author Ali Simpson here,
I'm a regular Cunarder so
hope you will enjoy this
novel, the first in a series.
If you like it, I hope you
will find me on Amazon and
leave me a review. Love Ali

Kitty and Nora Markham will return soon in

Death by Misdirection